지하촌

아시아에서는 《바이링궐 에디션 한국 대표 소설》을 기획하여 한국의 우수한 문학을 주제별로 엄선해 국내외 독자들에게 소개합니다. 이 기획은 국내외 우수한 번역가들이 참여하여 원작의 품격을 최대한 살렸습니다. 문학을 통해 아시아의 정체성과 가치를 살피는 데 주력해 온 아시아는 한국인의 삶을 넓고 깊게 이해하는 데 이 기획이 기여하기를 기대합니다.

Asia Publishers presents some of the very best modern Korean literature to readers worldwide through its new Korean literature series 〈Bilingual Edition Modern Korean Literature〉. We are proud and happy to offer it in the most authoritative translation by renowned translators of Korean literature. We hope that this series helps to build solid bridges between citizens of the world and Koreans through a rich in-depth understanding of Korea.

바이링궐 에디션 한국 대표 소설 090
Bi-lingual Edition Modern Korean Literature 090

The Underground Village

강경애

지하촌

Kang Kyŏng-ae

ASIA
PUBLISHERS

Contents

지하촌

The Underground Village

해는 서산 위에서 이글이글 타고 있다.

칠성이는 오늘도 동냥자루를 비스듬히 어깨에 메고 비틀비틀 이 동리 앞을 지났다. 밑 뚫어진 밀짚모자를 연신 내려쓰나 이마는 따갑고 땀방울이 흐르고 먼지가 연기같이 끼어 그의 코밑이 매워 견딜 수 없다.

"이애 또 온다."

"어아."

동리서 놀던 애들은 소리를 지르며 달려 나온다. 칠성이는 조놈의 자식들을 또 만나누나 하면서 속히 걸었으나, 벌써 애들은 그의 옷자락을 툭툭 잡아당겼다.

The sun was burning above the western hill. Ch'il-sŏng, as usual, staggered past this village with his beggar's sack slung over his shoulder. He kept pulling down his crownless straw hat, but the sun continued to scorch his forehead, and drops of sweat rolled down. Dust rose up from the parched road like smoke and made it difficult for him to breathe.

"There he comes again!"

"Come on!"

The little urchins at play by the roadside shouted and ran toward him. Ch'ilsŏng swore to himself and took hurried steps, but the children soon overtook him and pulled at his clothes.

"이애 울어라 울어."

한 놈이 칠성의 앞을 막아서고 그 큰 입을 헤벌리고 웃는다. 여러 애들은 즉 돌아섰다.

"이애 이애, 네 나이 얼마?"

"거게 뭐 얻어 오니? 보자꾸나."

한 놈이 동냥자루를 툭 잡아채니 애들은 손뼉을 치며 좋아한다. 칠성이는 우뚝 서서 그중 큰 놈을 노려보고 가만히 서 있었다. 앞으로 가려든지 또 욕을 건네면 애들은 더 흥미가 나서 달라붙는 것임을 잘 알기 때문이다.

"바루 바루 점잖은데."

머리 뺀죽 나온 놈이 나무 꼬챙이로 갓 눈 듯한 쇠똥을 찍어들고 대들었다. 여러 놈은 깔깔거리면서 저마다 쇠똥을 찍어 들고 덤볐다. 칠성이도 여기는 참을 수 없어서 막 서두르며 내달아 갔다.

두 팔을 번쩍 들고 부르르 떨면서 머리를 비틀비틀 꼬다가 한 발 지척 내디디곤 했다. 애들은 이 흉내를 내며 따른다. 앞으로 막아서고 뒤로 따르면서 깡충깡충 뛰어 칠성의 얼굴까지 쇠똥칠을 해놓는다. 그는 눈을 부릅뜨고,

"Cry, lad, cry!" One of the urchins blocked Ch'il-sŏng's way and laughed. The children surrounded him in a circle.

"Hey, boy, how old are you?"

"Show us what you earned today."

One of the urchins snatched at his beggar's sack, and all the others clapped their hands. Ch'ilsŏng stood immobile and glared at the biggest of the group. He knew that if he tried to push ahead or swore at them they would pester him still more.

"Oh, he looks like a gentleman today." One bris-tly-haired urchin brandished before his face a stick with a bit of cowdung at the tip. The children all giggled and made as if to smear cowdung on Ch'il-sŏng with their sticks.

Ch'ilsŏng could not stand it, so he ran as fast as he could.

He raised both his shaky arms high and twisted his neck convulsively as he placed one foot ahead of the other. The children mimicked his gait and followed him. They blocked him in front and be-hind, and jumped up to smear cowdung on his face. He scowled fiercely, and could only mutter "Goddamn!" after twitching his mouth for a long time.

"이 이놈들."

입을 실룩실룩 하다가 겨우 내놓은 말이다. 애들은,

"이 이놈들"

하고 또한 흉내를 내고는 대굴대굴 굴면서 웃는다. 쇠똥이 그의 입술에 올라가자, 앱 투 하고 침을 뱉으면서 무섭게 눈을 떴다.

"무섭다, 바루 바루."

애들은 참말 무섭게 보았는지 슬금슬금 꽁무니를 빼기 시작하였다. 칠성이는 팔로 입술을 비비치고 떠들며 돌아가는 애들을 물끄러미 바라보았다. 웬일인지 자신은 세상에서 버림을 받은 듯 그렇게 고적하고 분하였다.

그들이 물러간 후에 신작로는 적적하고 죽 뻗어 나가다가 조밭을 끼고 조금 굽어진 저 앞이 뚜렷했다. 그 위에 수수밭 그림자 서늘하고…… 그는 걸었다. 옷에 묻은 쇠똥을 털었으나, 떨어지지 않을 뿐 아니라 퍼렇게 물이 든다. 그는 어디라 없이 멍하니 바라보다가, 산 밑으로 와서 주저앉았다.

긴 풀에 잔바람이 훌훌히 감기고 이따금 들리는 벌레소리, 어디 샘물이 있는가 싶었다. 그는 보기 싫게 돋은

The children imitated the mouth and the "God-damn!" and roared with laughter. When cowdung touched his lips Ch'ilsŏng spat vehemently and scowled fiercely.

"Why, that's a terrible gentleman there," the children mocked, but perhaps they thought he really looked terrible, for they began to retreat. Ch'ilsŏng wiped his mouth with his sleeve and looked at the noisily retreating children. He felt furious and forlorn, like one cast aside by the world.

After the urchins had gone away, there was utter silence. Ch'ilsŏng walked on along the new highway. He tried to brush away the cowdung, but the effort only spead the bluish stain on his clothes. He stared into space, and flopped down on the slope at the foot of the mountain.

A breeze stirred the tall grasses, and insects chirped now and then. A running brook sang from somewhere, too. He scratched his head and looked ahead absently. The sun showered its oblique rays upon the forest, and the songs of the birds sounded plaintive. "Why am I such a cripple, that I am ridiculed and persecuted even by little children?" he pondered, and plucked a blade of grass beside him, which hurt his palm.

머리를 벅벅 긁어당기며 무심히 앞을 보았다. 수림 속에 햇발이 길게 드리웠고 짹짹 하는 새소리 처량하게 들렸다. 난 왜 병신이 되어 그놈의 새끼들한테까지 놀림을 받나 하고 불쑥 생각하면서 곁의 풀대를 북 뽑았다. 손목은 찌르르 울렸다.

큰년이가 살까! 그는 눈이 멀고도 사는데 난 그보다야 훨씬 낫지. 강아지의 털같이 보드라운 털을 가진 풀 열매를 바라보며 이렇게 생각하였다. 큰년이가 천천히 떠오른다. 곱게 감은 눈, 고것 참! 그는 진저리를 쳤다. 그리고 곁에 놓인 동냥자루를 보면서 오늘 얻어온 것 중에 가장 맛있고 좋은 것으로 큰년에게 보내야지 하였다. 어떻게 보낼까. 밤에 바자위로 넘겨줄까. 큰년이가 나와 바자 곁에 서 있어야 되지. 그럼 누가 나오라고는 해둬야지. 누구가 그래. 안 되어. 그럼 칠운이 들여서 보내지. 아니 아니, 안 되어. 큰년의 어머니가 알게 되고, 또 우리 어머니 알지. 안 되어. 낮에 김들 매러 간 담에 몰래 바자로 넘겨주지. 그는 가슴이 설레어서 부시시 일어나고 말았다.

가죽을 벗겨낼 듯이 내려 쪼이던 해도 어느덧 산 속

"Well, at least I'm not as miserable as Kŭnnyŏn," he thought. "Kŭnnyŏn is blind yet she lives," he mused, looking at the down-covered berries of a nearby plant. He pictured Kŭnnyŏn in his head. Her softly closed eyes! He trembled as he pictured them. He looked at his beggar's sack beside him and thought he would give Kŭnnyŏn the most delicious unbroken biscuits that he had garnered that day. "How shall I give them to her? Shall I hand them to her over the brushwood hedge tonight? To do so, Kŭnnyŏn will have to be made to come out and stand beside the brushwood hedge. Someone will have to tell her to come out. Who? No, that won't do. Then I will send Ch'il-un over with them. Oh, no, that way Kŭnnyŏn's mother and my mother will know. I will hand them over the hedge tomorrow at midday after people have gone out for weeding." His heart throbbed, and he got up.

The sun that had been pouring down heat as if to fry his skin disappeared among the mountains, and a cool breeze from somewhere stirred the grasses and cooled his body. Ch'ilsŏng fumbled with his beggar's sack and then, slinging it over his shoulder, resumed his tottering walk.

으로 숨어버리고, 어디선가 불어오는 바람이 풀잎을 살랑살랑 흔들고 그의 몸에 스며든다. 그는 동냥자루를 매만지다가, 어깨에 메고 지척하고 발길을 내디디었다.

하늘은 망망한 바다와 같이 탁 터져버리고, 저 멀리 붉은 놀이 유유히 떠돌고 있다. 그는 밀짚모자를 젖혀 쓰고 산밑을 떠났다. 걸음에 따라 쇠똥내가 물씬하고 났다.

그가 산모롱이를 돌아 동리 앞까지 왔을 때 그의 동생인 칠운이가 아기를 업고 쪼루루 달려온다.

"성 이제 오네. 히, 자꾸자꾸 봐도 안 오더니."

큰 눈에 웃음을 북실북실 띠우고 형의 곁으로 다가서는 칠운이는 시꺼먼 동냥자루를 덤썩 쥐어 무엇을 얻어온 것을 어서 알려고 하였다.

"오늘도 과자 얻어 왔어?"

"아 아니."

칠성이는 얼른 동냥자루를 옮기고 주춤 물러섰다. 칠운이는 따라 섰다.

"나 하나만 응야, 성아."

침을 꿀떡 넘기고 새카만 손을 내민다. 그 바람에 아

The sky spread before his eyes like a vast sea, and far off toward the horizon a red evening glow spread in waves. He pushed up his straw hat and came out of the shadows of the valley. As he moved, the smell of cowdung stung his nostrils.

When he had passed the mountain and approached the entrance to the village, his younger brother Ch'il-un ran up to him with the baby on his back.

"Oh, you're late. I've been waiting for you all day." His big eyes beaming happily, Ch'il-un went up close to his brother and, taking hold of the beggar's sack, tried to find out what he had obtained that day.

"Did you get biscuits today, too?"

Ch'il-un moved with him.

"Give me one, will you? Just one." Ch'il-un swallowed and stretched out his soiled hand. The baby on his back also spread both her hands and looked at Ch'ilsŏng.

"Goddamn!" Ch'ilsŏng turned away quickly. Ch'il-un followed him hastily.

"Will you, please? Give me one."

"I haven't got any." Ch'ilsŏng scowled. Ch'il-un became tearful at once and looked up at his broth-

기까지 두 손을 쪽 펴들고 칠성이를 말뚝히 쳐다본다.

"이 이 새끼는."

칠성이는 홱 돌아섰다. 칠운이는 넘어질 듯이 쫓아갔다.

"응야 성아, 나 하나만."

"없 없어!"

형은 눈을 치떴다. 칠운이는 금세 눈물이 글썽글썽해서 형을 보았다.

"난 어마이 오면 이르겠네 씨, 도무지 안 준다고, 아까 아까 어마이가 밭에 가면서 아기 보라면서 저 성이 사탕 얻어다 준다고 했는데 씨, 난 안 준다고 다 일러 씨, 흥." 칠운이는 입을 비쭉 하더니 주먹으로 눈물을 씻는다. 아기는 영문도 모르고 "으아" 하고 울음을 내쳤다.

주위는 감실감실 어두워 오는데 칠운이는 흑흑 느껴 울면서 그들의 어머니가 올라가 있을 저 산을 바라고 뛰어간다.

"어머이 어머이!"

하고 칠운이는 목메어 부르면 번번히 아기도,

"엄마 엄마!"

er.

"I'll tell Mother you won't give me a biscuit. She said when she went out to the field that if I looked after the baby you'd give me sweets. I'll tell on you, I will." Ch'il-un twisted his mouth and wiped his tears with his fist.

The baby, without knowing what it was all about, also began to cry. Darkness was setting in, but Ch'il-un sobbed and ran toward the mountain where their mother was supposed to be.

"Mother! Mother!" When Ch'il-un shouted sobbingly, the baby also cried "Mama! Mama!" The echo from the mountain sounded somewhat like their mother's reply of "Coming!" Ch'ilsŏng, deeming it fortunate to be rid of Ch'il-un and Yong-ae, turned and began to walk.

The village was sunk in darkness and nothing could be discerned, but the old locust tree loomed tall and erect, as if it were trying to reach the stars. He walked on, resolving that he would meet Kŭnnyŏn by whatever means, and give her the biscuits without fail.

"Is it you, Ch'ilsŏng?" It was his mother's voice. He looked back. Her face could not be seen under the big bundle of brushwood, which made her

하고 또랑또랑히 불렀다. "응응" 하는 앞산의 반응은 어찌 들으면 어머니의 "왜" 하는 대답 같기도 했다. 칠성이는 칠운이와 영애가 보이지 않는 것으로만 다행으로 돌아서 걸었다.

동네는 어둠에 폭 싸여 아무것도 보이지 않으나 동네 앞으로 우뚝 서 있는 늙은 홰나무만이 별을 따려는 듯 높아 보였다. 그는 이제 어떻게 해서라도 큰년이를 만날 것과 또 얻어 오는 이 과자를 큰년의 손에 꼭 쥐어줄 것을 생각하며 걸었다.

"칠성이냐?"

어머니의 음성이 들린다. 그는 돌아보았다. 나무를 한 짐 이고 이리로 오는 어머니의 얼굴은 보이지 않으나 웬일인지 그의 머리가 숙여지는 듯해서 번쩍 머리를 들었다.

"왜 오늘 늦었냐?"

아까 밭에서 산으로 올라갈 때 몇 번이나 아들이 나오는가 하여 눈이 가물가물해지도록 읍 길을 바라보아도 안 보이므로, 어디가 넘어져 애를 쓰는가? 또 애새끼들한테서 돌팔매질을 당하는가 하여 읍에까지 가볼까

neck tilt almost to the point of breaking.

"Why are you so late today?" She had looked down the road again and again to see if her son was coming until her eyes began to ache, and then had gone up the mountain from the field. She had worried that he might have fallen down somewhere or been stoned by urchins, and had thought of going to town in search of him. At his mother's question Ch'ilsŏng recalled the mortification he had received from the urchins and at once became tearful.

His mother walked up to him. She smelt of leaves. She was carrying the big sheaf of twigs on her head and also the baby on her back.

"Mother, he won't give me any sweets." Ch'il-un hung on to his mother's skirt. His mother staggered, almost fell down, but recovered her balance and stroked Ch'il-un with one hand.

"I'll kill that damned boy." Ch'ilsŏng raised his foot to kick his brother. His mother lurched in between them.

"Don't! He's had a hard time all day, looking after the baby. He's got heat rash all around his waist." Then his mother sighed deeply. Ch'ilsŏng suddenly fancied he smelt cowdung and his anger rose. "Do

하였던 것이다. 칠성이는 어머니의 이 같은 물음에 애들에게 쇠똥칠 당하던 것이 불시에 떠오르고 코허리가 살살 간지럽기 시작하였다.

어머니는 갈잎내를 확 풍기면서 그의 곁으로 다가선다. 그 큰 임을 이고도 아기까지 둘러업었다.

"어마이, 나 사탕. 성은 안 준다야 씨."

칠운이는 어머니의 치맛귀를 잡고 늘어진다. 그 바람에 어머니는 앞으로 쓰러질 듯했다가 도로 서서 한 손으로 칠운이를 어루만졌다.

"저놈의 새 새끼, 주 죽이고 말라."

칠성이는 발길로 칠운이를 차려 했다. 어머니는 또 쓰러질 듯 막아섰다.

"그러지 말어라. 원 그것이 해종일 아기 보느라 혼났다. 허리엔 땀띠가 좁쌀알같이 쪽 돋았단다. 여북 아프겠니 원."

어머니는 말끝에 한숨을 푹 쉰다. 칠성이는 문득 쇠똥내를 물큰 맡으면서 화를 버럭 올리었다.

"누 누구는 가 가만히 앉아 있었나!"

"아니 그렇게 하는 말이 아니어, 칠성아."

you think I've been sitting in the shade all day?"

"Oh, that's not what I meant, Ch'ilsŏng!" His mother's voice choked and she could not go on. They walked in silence.

When they got home they sat down on the sheaf of twigs. His mother talked about this and that to divert Ch'ilsŏng.

"Oh, there are so many stinging insects this year. My hands are all numb from their stings." She would have liked to take a look at her hands, but restrained herself and caressed the baby. She bared one of her breasts. Ch'il-un kicked at the bundle and went on whimpering. Ch'ilsŏng could not stand to look at his mother and sister, so he got up and looked around in the dark to see if Kŭnnyŏn was somewhere around.

Entering the room, Ch'ilsŏng sat down crosslegged, pressing under his thigh the toe he had bruised on the stepping stone, and noiselessly latched the door. Then he poured out the contents of the beggar's sack. Matchsticks and rice grains scattered with a rustling sound. He winced and rapidly felt the things one by one. He thought of the money that was in the sack, so he took it out and looked down at it absently. Nothing could be discerned

어머니는 목이 메어 다시 말을 계속하지 못한다. 그들은 잠잠히 걸었다.

집에 온 그들은 나뭇단 위에 되는대로 주저앉았다. 어머니는 칠성의 맘을 위로하느라고 이말 저말 끄집어냈다.

"올해는 웬 살쐐기 그리 많으냐. 손이 얼벌벌하구나."

어머니는 그 손을 한 번쯤 들여다보고 싶은 것을 참고, 아기를 어루만지다가 젖을 꺼냈다. 칠운이는 나뭇단을 통통 차면서 흥흥거린다. 칠성이는 동생들이 미워서 더 앉아 있을 수가 없어 일어났다. 그는 어둠 속을 휘살피고 큰년이가 저 속에 어디 섰지 않는가 했다.

방으로 들어온 칠성이는 이제 툇돌에 움찔린 발가락을 엉덩이로 꼭 눌러 앉고 일변 칠운이가 들어오지 않는가 귀를 기울이며 문을 걸었다.

그리고 동냥자루를 가만히 쏟았다.

흩어지는 성냥과 쌀알 흐르는 소리. 솜털이 오싹 일어 그는 몸을 움찔하면서 얼른 손을 내밀어 하나하나 만져보았다. 역시 거지 안에 있는 돈 생각이 나서 돈마저 꺼내 가지고 우두커니 들여다보았다. 비록 방 안이 어두워서 그 모든 것들이 보이지는 않으나 눈꼽같이 눈구석

clearly because the room was dark, but he imagined he could see everything distinctly.

He piled up the matchboxes and the rice and the biscuits separately in a corner and thought of Kŭnnyŏn. What should he give her? He picked up the biscuits quickly and, thinking that he would give her those, put one in his mouth. It crushed with a crisp sound between his teeth, and sweetness spread in his mouth. He smacked his lips and listened again to make sure Ch'il-un was not eavesdropping

He counted the money held tightly in his hand and, when he thought how happy Kŭnnyŏn would be if he used it to buy her fabrics for her clothes, his heart beat wildly. "Why doesn't she come to visit us at home? If she does, I'd give her money and biscuits and everything she wants." When he imagined her visiting them, he felt somehow reverential. So he wrapped the matchboxes and biscuits together and put them under the straw mat, pushing the money in under the mat too, and moved the rice near to the kitchen. Then, sitting beside the back door, he looked over at the hedge of Kŭnnyŏn's house.

Squash vines were winding round the hedge and

에 박혀 있는 듯했다.

성냥갑 따로, 쌀과 과자 부스러기 따로 골라 놓고, 문득 큰년이를 생각하였다. 어느 것을 주나, 얼른 과자를 쥐며, 이것을 주지하고 하나 집어 입에 넣었다. 바작 소리가 이 사이에 돌고 달큼한 물이 사르르 흐른다. 그는 입맛을 다시고 나서 칠운이가 엿듣는가 다시 한 번 조심했다.

그는 왼손에 땀이 나도록 쥐고 있는 돈을 펴서 보고 한푼 두푼 세어 보다가, 이것으로 큰년이의 옷감을 끊어다 주면 얼마나 큰년이가 좋아할까. 그의 가슴은 씩씩 뛰었다. 고것, 왜 우리 집엘 안 올까? 오면 내가 돈두 주고 이 과자도 주고, 또 또 큰년이가 달라는 것이면 내 다 주지 응 그래, 이리 생각되자 그는 어쩐지 맘이 송구해졌다. 해서 성냥갑과 과자 부스러기를 한데 싸서 저편 갈자리 밑에 밀어 넣고, 돈은 거지에 넣은 담에 쌀만 아랫방에 내려놨다. 그리고 뒷문 곁으로 바싹 다가앉아서 큰년네 바자를 바라다보았다.

바자에 호박넝쿨이 엉키었고 그 위에 벌들이 팔팔 날았다. 어떻게 만날까, 그는 무심히 발가락을 쥐고 아픔

stars were floating above it. "How can I meet her?" His hand touched his toe and it hurt. A cool breeze caressed his cheeks. His heart ached. It ached more than his bruised toe. "Eat your supper."

Ch'ilsŏng looked up, startled. When he realized it was his mother who was standing outside the door, he felt an emptiness in a corner of his bosom.

"Did you lock the door?" His mother pulled at the door. He felt as if she were pulling at the door to ask for biscuits or for money. He thought he hated his family and everybody in the world.

"I won't eat," he shouted. His whole body shook.

"Did you eat something in the market?" His mother's voice grew weak. Every time Ch'ilsŏng got angry, his mother's voice became weak like that. After a long interval, his mother pleaded again, "Why don't you have some more?"

"I don't want to," he shouted again. His mother murmured something to herself and fell silent. Ch'ilsŏng, left alone, yearned to eat the biscuits under the straw mat. He lifted it. A sweet scent floated up and also the disgusting smell of bedbugs. He replaced the straw mat and turned around, thinking that the biscuits must go to Kŭnnyŏn tomorrow,

을 느꼈다. 서늘한 바람이 그의 볼 위에 흘러내렸다. 그는 안타까웠다. 지금 이 발끝이 아픈 것보다도 어딘가 모르게 또 아픈 데가 있다는 것을 느낀다.

"이애 밥 먹어."

칠성이는 놀라 돌아보았다. 어머니가 샛문 밖에 서 있다는 것을 알자 웬일인지 가슴 한구석에 공허를 아뜩하게 느꼈다.

"왜 문은 걸었나."

어머니는 문을 잡아챈다. 과자를 달라거나 돈을 달래려고 저리도 문을 잡아 흔드는 것 같다. 그는 와락 미운 생각이 치올랐다.

"난 난 안 먹어!"

꽥 소리쳤다. 전신이 후루루 떨린다.

"장에서 뭐 먹고 왔니."

어머니의 음성은 가늘어진다. 언제나 칠성이가 화를 낼 땐 어머니는 저리도 기운이 없어진다. 한참 후에,

"좀 더 먹으렴."

"시 싫어."

역시 소리를 질렀다. 그러니 어머니는 뭐라구 웅설웅

but his hand was again fingering the mat. "I'll give them to Kŭnnyŏn." He took his hand away quickly and grabbed the doorsill.

A breeze squeezed in through the gap between the door panels and chilled his sweaty brow. He quickly took off his jacket and hugged the wind. He felt itchy all over, so he rubbed his body against the wall. It made him feel good, so he kept on doing it harder. That made him breathless, and the skin on his back tore and ached. So he got up, clinging to the wall, and went outside.

As he moved, every part of his body ached. His fingertip hurt as if pierced by a thorn, and his wrist ached and his arm felt sore and his toe stung. He ignored them all and walked on.

Among the onions planted in orderly rows beside the bush clover hedge a few white flowers shone like stars, and the smell of scallions that drifted with the wind made him feel as if a girl were sitting beside him. He stepped nearer to the hedge.

From Kŭnnyŏn's house floated the poignant smell of mugwort burning to keep away mosquitoes, and the fire itself flickered now and then. As he pricked his ears toward the conversation in Kŭnnyŏn's yard, the hedge rustled and the furry spines of squash

설하더니 잠잠해 버린다. 칠성이는 우두커니 앉았노라니 자꾸만 갈자리 속에 넣어둔 과자가 먹고 싶어 가만히 갈자리를 들썩하였다. 먼지내 싸하게 올라오고 빈대 냄새 역하다. 그는 갈자리를 도로 놓고 내일 아침에 큰년이 줄 것인데 내가 먹으면 안 되지 하고 휙 돌아앉고도 부지중에 손은 갈자리를 어루쓸고 있다. 큰년이 줘야지. 냉큼 손을 떼고 문턱을 꽉 붙들었다.

마침 바람이 산들산들 밀려들어 이마에 흐른 땀을 선뜻하게 한다. 그는 얼른 적삼을 벗어 던지고 그 바람을 안았다. 온몸이 가려운 듯하여 벽에다 몸을 비비치니 어떤 쾌미가 일어, 부지중에 그는 몸을 사정없이 비비치고 나니 숨이 차고 등가죽이 벗겨져 아팠다. 그래서 벽을 붙들고 일어나 나왔다.

몸을 움직이니 아니 아픈 곳이 없다. 손끝에 가시가 박혔는지 따끔거리고 팔뚝이 쓰라리고 아까 다친 발가락이 새삼스러이 더 쏘고, 그는 꾹 참고 걸었다.

울바자 밑에 나란히 서 있는 부초종 끝에 별빛인가도 의심나게 흰 꽃이 다문다문 빛나고 간혹 맡을 수 있는 부초 냄새는 계집이 곁에 와 섰는가 싶게 야릇했다. 그

leaves stung his cheeks. His face burned when he suddenly thought Kŭnnyŏn might be listening to his movements.

After a long while he looked around. His clothes were all damp with dew, and scallion blossoms shone like pebbles under water. The mosquito fire could not be seen any more, and all around was darkness. From somewhere insects chirped. When he stepped into his room he felt stuffiness fill his chest up to his throat.

When he awoke the next morning, the backyard was full of sunshine already. As soon as he got up, Ch'ilsŏng looked around to see whether his mother and Ch'il-un were in the house still. Making sure that they were not, he sat on the doorsill and looked at the hedge of Kŭnnyŏn's house. Kŭnnyŏn's father and mother must have gone out to the field to weed, and Kŭnnyŏn must be home alone.

"Could there be some visitor? I must see her today." Thinking thus, he looked down at his arms, which hung limp inside the tattered sleeves and looked as if they were made of no bones and no flesh, but only shrivelled greenish-yellow skin. Suddenly he felt sad and, raising his head, sighed deeply. How fortunate it was that Kŭnnyŏn was

는 바자 곁으로 다가섰다.

큰년네 집에선 모깃불을 피우는지 향긋한 쑥내가 솔솔 넘어오고 이따금 모깃불이 껌벅껌벅하는데 두런두런하는 소리에 그는 귀를 세우니 바자가 바삭바삭 소리를 내고 호박잎의 솜털이 그의 볼에 따끔거린다. 문득 그는 바자 저편에 큰년이가 숨어서 나를 엿보지나 않나 하자 얼굴이 확확 달았다.

어느 때인가 되어 가만히 둘러보니 옷에 이슬이 촉촉하였고 부초꽃이 물속에 잠긴 차돌처럼 그 빛을 환히 던지고 있다. 모깃불도 보이지 않고 캄캄하며, 어디선가 벌레 소리가 쓰르릉 하고 났다. 그는 방으로 들어서자 가슴이 답답하였다.

이튿날 아침에 눈을 뜨니 벌써 뒤뜰은 햇빛으로 가득하였다. 칠성이는 일어나는 참 어머니와 칠운이가 아직도 집에 있는가 살핀 담에 아무도 없음을 알고 뒷문턱에 걸터앉아서 큰년네 바자를 물끄러미 바라보았다. 큰년의 아버지 어머니도 김매러 갔을 테고 고것 혼자 있을 터인데…….

혹 마을꾼이나 오지 않았는지 오늘은 꼭 만나야 할

blind! If she could see, she would have taken to her heels at the sight of these arms. But what if Kŭnnyŏn felt these arms and asked why they were so thin and limp? And what one could do with such weak arms? His heart tore at the thought. He kept heaving sighs and suddenly thought, "Couldn't there be a medicine for them? There must be some medicine." On the spider's web spread over the hedge of Kŭnnyŏn's house hung innumerable dewdrops. "Maybe those are medicine." He sprang up and went outside.

Praying that the dewdrops shining on the spider's web would be medicine for him, he pulled the web down carefully. His arms were weak and trembled, so that the dewdrops fell on the ground in a shower. He tried to catch them in his palms, but not a drop fell on them.

"Goddamn!"

He had a habit of swearing "Goddamn" and glaring at the sky whenever he failed at something. As he was standing thus fuming to himself he turned his head at the soft sound of rubber shoes. The furry squash leaves touched his eyelids and he became tearful. Kŭnnyŏn seen through tears! He suppressed his urge to rub his eyes and opened them

터인데, 이런 생각을 하다가 무심히 그의 팔을 들여다 보았다. 다 해진 적삼소매로 맥없이 늘어진 팔목은 뼈도 살도 없고 오직 누렇다 못해서 푸른빛이 도는 가죽만이 있을 뿐이다. 갑자기 슬픈 마음이 들어 그는 머리를 들고 한숨을 푹 쉬었다. 큰년이가 눈을 감았기로 잘했지, 만일 두 눈이 동글하게 띄웠다면 이 손을 보고 십리나 달아날 것도 같다. 그러나 큰년이가 이 손을 만져보고 왜 이리 맥이 없어요, 이 손으로 뭘 하겠수 할 때엔…… 그는 가슴이 답답해서 견딜 수 없다. 그저 한숨만 맥없이 내쉬고 들이쉬다가 문득 약이 없을까? 하였다. 약이 있기는 있을 터인데…… 큰년네 바자 위에 둥글하게 심어 붙인 거미줄에는 수없는 이슬방울이 대롱대롱했다. 저런 것도 약이 될지 모르지, 그는 벌떡 일어나 밖으로 나왔다.

거미줄에서 빛나는 저 이슬방울들이 참으로 약이 되었으면 하면서, 그는 조심히 거미줄을 잡아당기려 했다. 팔은 맥을 잃고, 뿐만 아니라 자꾸만 떨리어 거미줄을 잡을 수도 없지만 바자만 흔들리고, 따라서 이슬방울이 후두두 떨어진다. 그는 손으로 떨어져 내려오는

wider.

Kŭnnyŏn, walking with a heavy wooden laundry basin on her head, came toward the hedge and, after putting the basin on the ground, straightened up. Her eyes were closed as if in sleep; or they seemed just slightly open. Perhaps from exertion, several red spots shone on her cheeks, and her chin seemed sharper than usual, making her look like someone who had been ill for days. Kŭnnyŏn shook the laundry piece by piece and spread it on the hedge. Ch'ilsŏng could not breathe. As he tried to inhale noiselessly, his heart felt about to burst and the skin of his belly contracted. He bowed down once to brush away his tears and kept looking. Nothing was in his head now except every movement of Kŭnnyŏn. Kŭnnyŏn came near him with her last piece of laundry. Ch'ilsŏng wanted to stretch out and take hold of Kŭnnyŏn's hand, but he flinched back instead, and his whole body shook.

As the hedge rustled under the spreading laundry, a thousand birds' wings flapped in his chest, sirens sang in his ears, and darkness descended on his eyes. He could move and part the squash leaves to look beyond the hedge only when

이슬방울을 받으려고 했다. 그러나 한 방울도 그의 손에는 떨어지지 않았다.

"에이, 비 빌어먹을 것!"

그는 이런 경우를 당할 때마다 이렇게 소리치고 말없이 하늘을 노려보는 버릇이 있다. 한참이나 이러하고 있을 때, 자박자박 하는 신발 소리에 그는 가만히 머리를 돌리어 바라보았다. 호박잎이 그의 눈썹 끝에 삭삭 비비치자 눈물이 핑그르르 돈다. 눈물 속에 비치는 저 큰년이! 그는 눈가가 가려운 것도 참고 눈을 점점 더 크게 떴다.

빨래 함지를 무겁게 든 큰년이는 이리로 와서 빨래 함지를 쿵 내려놓고 일어난다. 눈은 자는 듯 감았고 또 어찌 보면 감은 듯 뜬 것같이 보였다.

이제 빨래를 했음인지 양 볼의 붉은 점이 한 점 두 점 보이고 턱이 뾰족한 것이 어디 며칠 앓은 사람 같다. 큰년이는 빨래를 한 가지씩 들어 활짝 펴가지고 더듬더듬 바자에 넌다.

칠성이는 숨이 턱턱 막혀서 견딜 수 없다. 소리 나지 않게 숨을 쉬려니 가슴이 터지는 것 같고 뱃가죽이 다

Kŭnnyŏn's footsteps had retreated to a distance. Kŭnnyŏn was walking toward the kitchen door with the empty wooden basin on her head. He felt an urgent desire to call out to her and make her stop, but his voice would not function. Kŭnnyŏn's bare legs showed once or twice through the torn skirt and disappeared. He stared at the kitchen door, hoping that she would come out again, but she did not reappear. He heaved a deep sigh and came away from the hedge. The sun shone hot. He wished he had given her the biscuits. He wished he had given her the money. "No, I'll save the money and buy her material for a skirt," he thought, and peeped in again. Only the hedge rustled; otherwise all was silence. The laundry washed by Kŭnnyŏn shone so bright that he averted his eyes and turned away. If he didn't buy her clothes, Kŭnnyŏn would go around showing her legs through the torn skirt forever.

"Give me sweets, will you, please?"

He looked back to see Ch'il-un coming out of the kitchen door with the baby on his back. He moved away from the hedge like one discovered in theft. Ch'il-un, thinking that his brother was coming to beat him, ran into the kitchen, but looked

잡아씌웠다. 그는 잠깐 머리를 숙여 눈물을 씻어낸 후에 여전히 들여다보았다. 지금 그의 머리엔 아무런 생각도 할 수 없다. 그저 큰년의 동작으로 가득했을 뿐이다. 큰년이는 한 가지 남은 빨래를 마저 가지고 그의 앞으로 다가온다. 그때 칠성이는 손이라도 쑥 내밀어 큰년의 손을 덥석 잡아보고 싶었으나 몸은 움찔 뒤로 물러나지며 온 전신이 풀풀 떨리었다.

바삭바삭 빨래 널리는 소리가 칠성의 귓바퀴에 돌아내릴 때 가슴엔 웬 새 새끼 같은 것이 수없이 팔딱거리고 귀가 우석우석 울고 눈은 캄캄하였다. 큰년의 신발소리가 멀리 들릴 때 그는 비로소 몸을 움직일 수 있었고 또 호박잎을 젖히고 들여다보았다. 큰년이는 빈 함지를 들고 부엌문을 향하여 들어가고 있다. 그는 급하여 소리라도 쳐서 큰년이를 멈추고 싶었으나, 역시 맘뿐이었다. 큰년의 해어진 치마폭 사이로 빨건 다리가 두어 번 보이다가 없어진다. 또 나올까 해서 그 컴컴한 부엌문을 뚫어지도록 보았으나 끝끝내 큰년이는 나오지 않았다. 그는 후 하고 숨을 내쉬고 물러섰다. 햇볕은 따갑게 내려쬔다. 과자나 들려줄 걸…… 돈이나 줄 것

back and approached him again.

"Will you? Just one." He held out his hand.

The baby also tilted her head to look at her older brother, and spread out her hand. The baby's head was covered with sores which oozed all the time. The baby's thin, light-brown hair was pasted to the sores, and flies always swarmed around her head. The baby kept pulling at her hair with her tiny fingers and ate the scabs she tore from her head.

The baby held out that hand before her brother. She thrust her hand before her brother with fingers spread like a fan. Ch'ilsŏng scowled at them once and went into the room. Ch'il-un blocked the doorway and importunately begged again. "Will you? Give me just one and I'll go away." He snuffled up his snot.

"I don't want to see you!"

Ch'il-un had no shirt so he was clad only in a pair of pants. The skin of his back, parched and grilled by the sun, was peeling in flakes. The baby did not have even a pair of pants, so she was naked all the time. His eyes burned as he looked at the bare bodies of his younger brother and sister. As he turned his eyes to the wall, he pictured the pile upon pile of cloth stacked along the walls of the

을, 아니 돈은 내가 모았다가 치마나 해주지 하고 다시 들여다보았다. 바자만 바삭바삭 소리를 내고 고요하다. 이제 큰년의 손으로 넌 빨래는 희다 못해서 햇빛같이 빛나고 그는 눈을 떼고 돌아섰다. 자기가 옷가지라도 해주지 않으면 큰년이는 언제나 그 뻘건 다리를 감추지 못할 것 같다.

"성아, 나 사탕 좀."

돌아보니 칠운이가 아기를 업고 부엌문으로 나온다. 그는 도둑질이나 하다가 들킨 것처럼 무안해서 얼른 바자 곁을 떠났다. 칠운이는 저를 다그쳐 형이 저리도 급히 오는 것으로 알고 부엌으로 달아나다가 살짝 돌아보고 또 이리 온다.

"응야, 나 하나만……."

손을 내민다.

아기도 머리를 갸웃하여 오빠를 바라보고 손을 내민다. 아기의 조 머리엔 종기가 지질하게 났고, 거기에는 언제나 진물이 마를 사이 없다. 그 위에 가늘고 노란 머리카락이 이기어 달라붙었고 또 파리가 안타깝게 달라붙어 떨어지지 않는다. 아기는 자꾸 그 가는 손가락으

town store. His hand that had been raised to strike Ch'il-un fell limp.

"If you don't give me any, I won't look after the baby." Ch'il-un put down the baby and ran away. The baby began to cry, screaming. Ch'ilsŏng did not cast a glance at the baby, but turned away. Flies were swarming around the rice bowl. His mother always went out to the field after setting his rice and soup in the room under a cloth, because Ch'ilsŏng got up late. He went up to it and lifted the cloth. A drowned fly floated in the soup, and the countless flies that had been sitting on the rice flew up startled. He picked out the fly from the soup and put a spoonful of rice into his mouth. The food consisted of a little rice and many acorns. The scanty rice, when crushed between his teeth, was so soft and glutinous and sweet that it almost made him choke. But immediately the crunched acorns filled his mouth with bitter juice. He tried to swallow the acorns without chewing, but they did not go down his throat, lingering in his mouth and spreading bitterness.

When he looked a while later, the baby had already stopped crying and was crawling toward her brother. She looked at her brother and looked at

로 머리를 쥐어 당기고 종기 딱지를 떼어 오물오물 먹고 있다.

아기는 그 손을 오빠 앞에 쳐들었다. 손가락을 모을 줄 모르고 쫙 펴들고 조른다. 칠성이는 눈을 부릅떠 보이고 방으로 들어왔다. 칠운이는 문 앞에 딱 막아서서 훙훙거렸다.

"응야 성아, 한 알만 주면 안 그래."

시퍼런 코를 훌떡 들여 마신다.

"보 보기 싫다!"

칠운이 역시 옷이 없어 잠방이만 입었고 그래서 저 등은 햇볕에 타다 못해서 허옇게 까풀이 일고 있으며 아기는 그나마도 없어서 쫄[1] 벗겨 두었다. 동생들의 이러한 모양을 바라보는 그는 눈에서 불이 확확 일어난다. 눈을 돌리어 벽을 바라보자 문득 읍의 상점에 첩첩이 쌓인 옷감을 생각하였다. 그는 자기도 모르게 손을 번쩍 들어 칠운이를 치려 했으나 그 손은 맥을 잃고 늘어진다.

"난 그럼, 아기 안 보겠다야, 씨."

칠운이는 아기를 내려놓고 달아난다. 그러니 아기는

the rice bowl and then looked at her brother again. Ch'ilsŏng, as a reward for having stopped crying, sorted the rice grains in the bowl and gave the baby a spoonful. The baby swallowed the rice in no time and then looked up at her brother again. This time Ch'ilsŏng gave her an acorn. The baby did not put it into her mouth but kept fingering it.

He cursed loudly at the baby who could tell rice from acorn. The baby twisted her mouth and began to cry.

"Stop it!" Ch'ilsŏng kicked the baby. The baby closed her eyes tightly and lay prostrate on the floor. The flies on her head flew up once but settled down again immediately. When Ch'ilsŏng raised his foot again to kick, the baby just sniffled and stopped crying. But tears kept rolling out of her eyes. Ch'ilsŏng went on eating but turned his head at the sound of a choking cough.

The baby, who had eaten the acorn in the meantime, had vomited. The acorn thrown up with the baby's reddish saliva was not chewed at all. The reddish tint was of blood. The baby's face was flushed and muscles stood out on her neck.

Ch'ilsŏng instantly felt the acorn in his mouth taste like sand, and a bitter smell rose up. He flung

악을 쓰고 운다. 칠성이는 눈도 거들떠보지 않고 돌아앉아 파리가 우글우글 끓는 곳을 바라보니 밥그릇이 눈에 띄었다. 언제나 어머니는 그가 늦게 일어나므로 저렇게 밥바리에 보를 덮어놓고 김매러 가는 것이다. 그는 슬그머니 다가앉아 술을 들고 보를 들치었다. 국에는 파리가 빠져 둥둥 떠다니고 밥바리에 붙었던 수없는 강구[2)]떼는 기겁을 해서 달아난다. 그는 파리를 건져내고 밥을 푹 떠서 입에 넣었다. 밥이란 도토리뿐으로 밥알은 어쩌다가 씹히곤 했다. 씹히는 그 밥알이야말로 극히 부드럽고 풀기가 있으며 그 맛이 달큼해서 기침을 할 지경이었다. 그러나 그 맛은 잠깐이고 또 도토리가 미끈하고 씹혀 밥맛이 쓰디쓴 맛으로 변한다. 그래 도토리만은 잘 씹지 않고 우물우물해서 얼른 삼키려면 그만큼 더 넘어가지 않고 쓴 물을 뿌리며 혀끝에 넘나들었다.

얼마 후에 바라보니 아기가 언제 울음을 그쳤는지 눈이 보송보송해서 발발 기어오다가 오빠를 보고 멀거니 쳐다보다가는 그 눈을 밥그릇에 돌리곤 또 오빠의 눈치를 살핀다. 칠성이는 그 듣기 싫은 울음을 그친 것이 대

away his spoon, picked up the child, and put her down on the dirt floor. When he spanked the baby's fleshless buttocks, her face turned dark but she kept sobbing silently. He kicked the rice bowl and walked across the room. He could not bear to hear the vomiting sound. He remembered the biscuits underneath the mat and, taking them all out and throwing them down in front of the baby, went out into the backyard. He circled the yard for some time and spat.

When he came into the room again, it was hot like the inside of a stove. He kept standing up and sitting down, and when he turned his head to look he found the baby asleep on the dirt floor, head pillowed on hand. On her vomit flies were crawling, and on the baby's head and inside the baby's open mouth were swarms of flies. Biscuits! Startled, he looked. Not a morsel of the biscuits remained. The baby could not have eaten them all so fast. Ch'il-un must have been home. He regretted that he had given them all to the baby, and thought he would beat up Ch'il-un when he saw him. He ran outside, kicking the baby on his way. He hated to look at the baby lying on her side with one hand under her head like a grown-up, and he hated to

견해서 얼른 밥알을 골라 내쳐 주었다. 그러니 아기는 그 조그만 손으로 밥알을 쥐어 먹다가 성이 차지 않아서 납작 엎드리어서 밥알을 쫄쫄 핥아 먹고는 또 멀거니 오빠를 본다. 이번에는 도토리 알을 내쳐 주었다. 아기는 웬일인지 당길성 없게 도토리를 쥐고는 손으로 조물작조물작 만지기만 하고 먹지는 않는다.

"아, 안 먹게이!"

도토리를 분간해서 아는 아기가 어쩐지 미운 생각이 왈칵 들어 그는 이렇게 소리쳤다. 그러니 아기는 입을 비죽비죽하다가 으아 하고 울었다.

"우 울겠니?"

칠성이는 발길로 아기를 찼다. 아기는 눈을 꼭 감고 방바닥에 쓰러졌다. 그 바람에 아기 머리의 파리는 웅 하고 조금 떴다가 곧 달라붙는다.

칠성이는 재차 차려고 달려드니, 아기는 코만 풀찐풀찐하면서 울음소리를 뚝 끊었다. 그러나 그 눈엔 눈물이 샘솟듯 흐른다. 칠성이는 모른 체하고 돌아앉아 밥만 퍼먹다가 캑 하는 소리에 머리를 돌렸다.

아기는 언제 그 도토리를 먹었던지 캑캑하고 게워 놓

look at her thin limbs.

Hearing the baby's cry, he searched for Ch'il-un. Ch'il-un was playing with other children under the willow tree. He walked toward them, breathing hard. Although he walked as stealthily as he could, Ch'il-un caught sight of him and ran away. The children, chewing on Indian millet stalks, eyed Ch'ilsŏng and giggled. Some of them imitated Ch'ilsŏng's gait.

Ch'il-un could not be seen anywhere. When Ch'il-sŏng fell down because his foot caught in a vine, the children who had been following him laughed and chattered noisily. He stood up with difficulty and scowled at the children because he was afraid that they, too, might attack him in a body. The children, perhaps frightened by his scowl, took to their heels. To Ch'ilsŏng they did not look like children but a horde of hungry monkeys after prey. He stared at their backs, thinking that all the children of this village were hateful. His forehead burned in the sun and his toe stung. The husks of Indian millet stalks that the children had peeled off hurt the soles of his feet. The children were running toward the brook. He thought Ch'il-un must be among them, and went toward the willow tree.

There were more Indian millet husks around the

는다. 깨느르르한 침에 섞이어 나오는 도토리 쪽은 조금도 씹히지 않은 그대로였고 그 빛이 약간 붉은 기를 띤 것을 보아 피가 묻어 나오는 것임을 알 수가 있었다. 아기의 얼굴은 빨갛게 상기되고 목에 힘줄이 불쑥 일어났다.

그 찰나에 칠성이는 입에 문 도토리가 모래알 같아 씹을 수 없고, 쓴 내가 콧구멍 깊이 칵 올려받혀 견딜 수 없었다. 그는 술을 뎅겅 내치고 아기를 번쩍 들어 문 밖으로 내놓았다. 그리고 뼈만 남은 아기의 볼기를 짝 붙이니 얼굴이 새카매지면서도 여전히 윽윽 게운다. 이번에는 밥그릇을 냅다 차서 요란스레 굴리고 웃방으로 올라오나 게우는 소리에 몸이 오시러워서 가만히 있을 수 없었다. 문득 갈자리 속의 과자를 생각하고 그것을 남김없이 꺼내다가 아기 앞에 팽개치고 뒷뜰로 나와버렸다. 그는 빙빙 돌다가 침을 탁 뱉었다.

한참 만에 칠성이는 방으로 들어오니 방 안은 단 가마속 같았다.

그는 앉았다 섰다 안달을 하다가 머리를 기웃하여 보니 아기는 손을 깔고 봉당에 엎디어 잠들었고, 게워 놓

willow tree and cowdung was scattered here and there, because people tied their cows to the tree. He leaned against the tree and looked. Before he knew it, his eyes had turned to Kŭnnyŏn's house. He yearned to see Kŭnnyŏn again. She'd be alone at home now. But what if somebody was there? Something stung him. Several huge ants were crawling up his legs. He brushed them off and looked again.

Far away on the hedge of Kŭnnyŏn's house were spread white garments, looking as if they would fly up like birds at the faintest sound. "No," he said to himself, "Nobody's there. Everybody's gone weeding." At the sound of footsteps he looked back. Kaettong's mother was walking toward him heavily, carrying a woman on her back.

Normally when they met she would accost him jokingly, with banter such as "Have you earned many boxes of matches? How about making a present of one to me?" But today she passed him without a word, her face tearful. Sweat poured in torrents from her forehead, her legs tottered, and she was panting like mad. Ch'ilsŏng saw that the woman being carried on her back looked like a corpse. The disheveled hair, the foamy mouth, the

은 자리엔 쉬파리가 날개 없는 듯이 벌벌 기고 있으며, 아기 머리와 빠끔히 벌린 입에는 잔파리 왕파리가 아글바글 들싼다.

과자! 그는 놀라 둘러보았다. 부스러기도 볼 수 없었다. 아기가 다 먹을 수 없고 필시 칠운이가 들어왔던 것이라 생각될 때 좀 남기고 줄 것을 하는 후회가 일며 칠운이를 보면 실컷 때리고 싶었다. 그는 달아나오면서 발길로 아기를 차고 나왔다. 손을 거북스레 깔고 모로 누운 꼴이 눈에 꺼리고 또 여윈 팔다리가 보기 싫어서 이러하고 나온 것이다.

아기 울음소리를 들으면서 그는 칠운이를 찾았다. 저편 버드나무 아래에 애들이 모여 떠든다. 옳지 저게 있구나 하고 씩씩거리며 그리로 발길을 떼어 놓았다.

몰래몰래 오느라 했건만 칠운이는 벌써 형을 보고서 달아난다. 애들은 수수대를 시시하고 씹고 서서 칠성이를 힐끔힐끔 보다가는 히히 웃었다. 어떤 놈은 칠성의 걸음 흉내를 내기도 한다.

칠운이는 조밭으로 들어갔는지 보이지도 않는다. 그가 잡풀에 얽히어 넘어지니 뒤에 따르던 애들은 허 하

torn clothes. When he looked at the face inside the chaos of hair, he recognized Kŭnnyŏn's mother. He wanted to ask questions, but Kaettong's mother had already gone past the willow tree. What happened? Did she faint? Did she fight with somebody? He got up and followed them. He wanted to overtake Kaettong's mother and find out what was the matter, but his legs did not carry him as fast as he wished. He staggered even more than usual and did not advance much. He got angry, swerved wildly, and fell down. After writhing for a long time he got up and began walking slowly.

Smoke rose from Kŭnnyŏn's chimney. Oh, what had happened to Kŭnnyŏn's mother? As he went near Kŭnnyŏn's house, his feet moved toward it of their own accord, but he checked himself and walked round it, hoping to overhear something.

When he stepped into the dirt yard he saw the baby defecating in the midst of a swarm of flies. As she strained hard, her anus jutted out like a finger and red blood dropped from it. The baby's eyes were dilated to the full and muscles stood out on her face like the blade of a sword. The small forehead was dripping with sweat. Ch'ilsŏng averted his face and went into the room. He wished he could

고 웃고 떠든다.

칠성이는 겨우 일어나서 애들을 노려보았다. 이놈들도 달려들지나 않으려나 하는 불안이 약간 일어 이렇게 닥 버티어 보인 것이다. 애들은 무서웠던지 슬금슬금 달아난다. 애들 같지 않고 무슨 원숭이 무리가 먹을 것을 구하려 눈이 뒤집혀서 다니는 것 같았다. 이 동리 애들은 모두가 미운 애들만이라고 부지중에 생각되어 한참이나 바라보다가 걸었다. 이마가 따갑고 발가락이 따가운데 또 애들이 벗겨버린 수숫대 껍질이 발끝에 따끔거린다. 애들은 내를 바라보고 달아난다. 그 무리에 칠운이도 섞이었을 것이라 하고 그는 버드나무 아래로 왔다.

여기는 수숫대 껍질이 더 많고 또 소를 갖다 매는 탓인지 소똥이 늘어분했다. 버드나무에 기대서서 그는 바라보았다. 저절로 그의 눈이 큰년에 집에 멈추고 또 큰년이를 만나볼 맘으로 가득했다. 지금 혼자 있을 텐데 가볼까. 그러나 누가 있으면…… 무엇이 따끔하기에 보니, 왕개미 몇 마리가 다리로 올라온다. 그는 툭툭 털고 다시 보았다.

멀리 큰년에 바자엔 빨래가 희게 널렸는데 방금 날으

step on the baby and kill it or cast it away on a distant mountain.

Putting into his mouth the acorn his foot had kicked, and scowling fiercely at the baby's groans, he came out into the backyard. He remembered Kŭnnyŏn's mother again and stepped up to the hedge.

He raised his head at the sound of a baby crying. He recognized at once that it was not his sister but a new-born infant. He realized Kŭnnyŏn's mother must have delivered a baby. Then his anxiety subsided a little, but he felt a bitter taste in his mouth at the thought of a baby. He thought that babies had better be killed as soon as they were born rather than let live like his baby sister.

Had she given birth to a girl like Kŭnnyŏn again? A blind girl? He giggled for no reason at the thought. Before his giggle died down he wondered to himself why it was that the women of this village produced such deformed children. Well, Kŭnnyŏn wasn't blind from birth. And as for himself, he also became a cripple at four after suffering paralysis following the measles. Then he recalled what his mother always said about his illness.

At that time his mother went to the town hospital,

려는 새와 같이 되룩되룩하여 쉬 하면 푸르릉 날 듯하다. 있기는 누가 있어, 김매러 다 갔을 터인데…… 신발 소리에 그는 돌아보았다. 개똥 어머니가 어떤 여인을 무겁게 업고 숨이 차서 온다. 전 같으면 "요새 성냥 많이 벌었겠구먼, 한 갑 선사하게나." 하고 농담을 건넬 터인데 오늘은 울상을 하고 잠잠히 지나친다. 이마에 비지땀이 흐르고 다리가 비틀비틀 꼬이고 숨이 하늘에 닿고 그는 머리를 들어보니 등에 업힌 여인인즉 죽은 시체 같았다. 흩어진 머리 주제며 입에 끓는 거품 꼴, 피투성이 된 옷! 눈을 크게 뜨고 머리카락에 휩싸인 여인의 얼굴을 똑바로 보니 큰년의 어머니였다. 그는 놀랐다. 해서 뭐라고 묻고 싶은데 벌써 개똥 어머니는 버드나무를 지나 퍽이나 갔다. 웬일일까? 어디 넘어졌나, 누구와 쌈을 했나 하고 두루 생각하다가, 못 견디어 일어나 따랐다. 맘대로 하면 얼른 가서 개똥 어머니에게 어찌된 곡절을 묻겠는데 다리가 말을 듣지 않고 점점 더 비틀거리기만 하고 앞으로 가지지는 않는다. 그는 화를 더럭 내고 몸짓만 하다가 팍 거꾸러졌다. 한참이나 버둥거리다가 일어나서 천천히 걸었다.

walking miles in knee-deep snow, carrying him on her back. After waiting in vain for an eternity in the unheated hall in the hospital, she pushed open the door of the consultation room, but the doctor raised his eyebrows and motioned her out, so she went into the hall again and waited another eternity, till at last an errand boy came out with a finger-thin vial.

Whenever she recalled that day she cursed the doctor vehemently, and cursed the world, too. Whenever his mother talked about it Ch'ilsŏng always cut her short and told her not to say any more. He couldn't bear to listen to it.

"Would I get better if I took medicine? Would Kŭnnyŏn be all right if she took medicine? Oh, no. After you are crippled no medicine can cure you. But who knows? Maybe if I could take some good medicine I might be able to move my limbs freely like other people and go up the mountains to gather wood, and not be mocked by little urchins." He felt a heaviness in his chest. He opened his eyes. Shall I go to a hospital and inquire? "The doctors, they don't care about anything but money," he repeated his mother's words and flopped down on the ground.

큰년네 굴뚝에는 연기가 흐른다. 옳구나, 큰년의 어머니가 어찌해서 그 모양이 되었을까, 또다시 이러한 궁금증이 일어난다. 그가 큰년네 마당까지 오니 큰년네 집으로 들어가고 싶어 발길이 자꾸만 돌려진다. 그런 것을 참고 무슨 소리나 들을까 하여 한참이나 왔다 갔다 하다가 집으로 왔다.

봉당에 들어서니 파리가 와그그 끓는데, 그 속에서 아기가 똥을 누고 있다. 깽깽 힘을 쓰니, 똥은 안 나오고 밑이 손길같이 빠지고 거기서 빨간 핏방울이 똑똑 떨어진다. 아기는 기를 쓰느라 두 눈을 동그랗게 비켜 뜨니, 얼굴의 힘줄이 칼날같이 일어난다. 그 조그만 이마에 땀이 비오듯 하고. 그는 못 볼 것이나 본 것처럼 머리를 돌리고 방으로 들어왔다. 마음대로 하면 아기를 칵 밟아 죽여 버리든지 어디 멀리로 들어다 버리든지 했으면 오히려 시원할 것 같았다.

칠성이는 발길에 채어 구르는 도토리를 집어 먹으며 아기 기 쓰는 소리에 눈살을 잔뜩 찌푸리고 그만 뒤뜰로 나와 버렸다. 아기로 인하여 잠깐 잊었던 큰년 어머니의 생각이 또 나서, 그는 바자 곁으로 다가섰다.

Silence came from Kŭnnyŏn's house and the baby's crying had ceased. Ch'ilsŏng felt hungry. He looked at the sun and thought that when his mother came back presently she would look at him through her unkempt hair with anxiety and ask him why he hadn't gone out begging today, and what would they eat tomorrow? He looked at the bush clover trees.

"Could this bush clover tree be medicine for my disease?" he suddenly thought as he smelt the cool scent of the bush, and bit off a stalk. When he chewed on it, the smell of grass nauseated him and he felt like vomiting. But he closed his eyes tightly and chewed and swallowed without breathing. His throat felt torn, and saliva flowed and flowed. He thought the medicine would work only if he swallowed the saliva too, so he blinked his eyes and swallowed the saliva. For some reason tears flowed out of both his eyes.

He looked up at the sky and prayed that he would one day be able to gather wood instead of his mother. He had never had such a thought before; he didn't use to feel acutely sorry even when he saw his mother walking with difficulty under a big bundle of wood, but somehow he prayed such

"으아 으아."

하는 아기 울음소리에 머리를 돌렸다. 영애의 울음소리가 아니요, 아주 갓난 어린 아기의 울음인 것을 직각하자 큰년의 어머니가 아기를 낳았는가 했다. 그러니 불안하던 마음이 다소 덜리나 아기하고 입에만 올려도 입에서 신물이 돌 지경이었다. 지금 봉당에서 피똥을 누느라 병든 고양이 꼴 한 그런 아기를 낳을 바엔 차라리 진자리에서 눌러 죽여 버리는 것이 훨씬 나을 것 같았다.

큰년이 같은 그런 계집애를 낳았나, 또 눈먼 것을…… 그는 히 하고 웃음이 터졌다. 그 웃음이 입가에서 사라지기도 전에 왜 이 동네 여인들은 그런 병신만을 낳을까? 하니, 어쩐지 이상하였다. 하기야 큰년이가 어디 나면서부터 눈멀었다니, 우선 나도 네 살 때에 홍역을 하고 난 담에 경풍이라는 병에 걸리어 이런 병신이 되었다는데 하자, 어머니가 항상 외우던 말이 생각되었다.

그때 어머니는 앓는 자기를 업고 눈이 성같이 쌓여 길도 찾을 수 없는 데를 눈 속에 푹푹 빠지면서 읍의 병원에를 갔다는 것이다. 의사는 보지도 못한 채 어머니

a prayer at that moment.

He stood perfectly still for a long while and then raised his arm before his eyes with a pounding heart. But the arm was still withered. He vomited suddenly and, hitting his head against the ground, began to weep.

It was after deep darkness had fallen that his mother came back, again with a load of wood.

"Are you sick?' The dim figure of his mother looked as if it would topple down any moment from the weight of fatigue. And the thick smell of grass, soaked through and through in her skirt, smelt like garlic.

"Dear, why don't you answer me?" His mother's hand as she touched him felt like a piece of log, but it had some warmth in it.

Ch'ilsŏng pushed away his mother's hand and turned away. His mother, sitting a few feet from him, studied her son and said, as if to herself, "Why doesn't he tell me if he's sick?" and got up and left the room. After some time his mother came in with rice boiled in vegetable soup and helped her son sit up. Ch'ilsŏng sat up and held the spoon with a trembling hand.

"Darling, are you sick?" Now his mother's clothes

는 난로도 없는 복도에 한겻[3]이나 서고 있다가, 하도 갑갑해서 진찰실 문을 열었더니 의사가 눈을 거칠게 떠보이고, 어서 나가 있으라는 뜻을 보이므로, 하는 수 없이 복도로 와서 해가 지도록 기다리는데 나중에 심부름하는 애가 나와서 어머니 손가락만한 병을 주고 어서 가라고 하였다는 것이다.

어머니는 그 말만 하면 흥분이 되어 의사를 욕하고 또 세상을 원망하는 것이다. 그때마다 그는 어머니를 핀잔하고 그 말을 막아버리곤 하였다. 무엇보다도 불쾌하여 견딜 수 없었던 것이다.

약만 먹으면 이제라도 내 병이 나을까, 큰년이 병도…… 아니야. 이미 병신이 된 담에야 약을 쓴다고 나을까, 그래도 알 수가 있나, 어쩌다 좋은 약만 쓰면 나도 남처럼 다리팔을 제대로 놀리고 해서 동냥도 하러 다니지 않고, 내 손으로 김도 매고 또 산에 가서 나무도 쾅쾅 찍어오고, 애새끼들한테서 놀림도 받지 않고…… 그의 가슴은 우쩍하였다. 눈을 번쩍 떴다. 병원에나 가서 물어볼까…… 그까짓 놈들이 돈만 알지 뭘 알아. 어머니의 하던 말 그대로 되풀이하고 맥없이 주저앉았다.

smelt of smoke, and with her breath came the smell of boiled rice. Ch'ilsŏng felt better.

"No."

His mother set her mind at ease and looked at her son eating soup.

"Kŭnnyŏn's mother had a baby today in the field. Oh, why do babies get born in poor homes?"

Ch'ilsŏng recalled the sight of Kŭnnyŏn's mother as he saw her under the willow tree, and the cry of the new-born infant rang in his ears. The miserable sight of Yong-ae as she tried to defecate revived before his eyes. He scowled.

"Oh, why should the likes of us conceive? Heaven's too unfeeling."

His mother sighed and went out with the empty bowl. Ch'ilsŏng, partly because it was too hot in the room and also because he wanted to know what was happening in Kŭnnyŏn's house, went outside.

From the pile of wood in a corner of the yard a strong smell of grass rose up, and the stars in the dark-blue sky shone like babies' eyes. He chased away the annoying mosquitoes and sat down on the heap of dry wood. Leaves rustled, and the warm mist rising from the wood warmed his bottom. His mother walked up to him.

큰년네 집도 조용하고 아기의 울음소리도 그쳤는데 배가 쌀쌀 고팠다. 그는 해를 짐작해 보고, 어머니가 이제 들어오면 얼굴에 수심을 띄우고 귀밑의 머리카락을 담뿍 흘리고서, 너 왜 동냥하러 가지 않았니, 내일은 뭘 먹겠니 할 것을 머리에 그리며 무심히 옆에 서 있는 댑싸리나무를 바라보았다.

혹시 이 댑싸리나무가 내 병에 약이 되지나 않을까, 그는 댑싸리나무 냄새를 코밑에 서늘히 느끼자, 이러한 생각이 불쑥 일어, 댑싸리나무 곁으로 가서 한입 뜯어 물었다. 잘강잘강 씹으니, 풀내가 역하게 일며 욱하고 구역질이 나온다. 그래도 눈을 꾹 감고 숨도 쉬지 않고 대강 씹어서 삼켰다. 목이 찢어지는 듯이 아프고 맑은 침이 자꾸만 흘러내린다. 그는 이 침마저 삼켜야 약이 될 듯해서 눈을 꿈쩍거리면서 그 침을 삼키고 나니, 까닭 없이 두 줄기 눈물이 주루루 흘러내린다.

그는 하늘을 바라보고 제발 이 손을 조금만이라도 놀려서 어머니가 하는 나무를 내가 하도록 하시사 하였다. 평소에 이런 생각을 한 번도 해본 적이 없건만, 어머니가 나무를 무겁게 이고 걸음도 잘 걷지 못하는 것을

"Is that you, Ch'ilsŏng? Why did you come out?" She sat down beside him and the wood rustled. Ch'il-sŏng averted his head because of the smell of sweat and baby's dung. His mother suckled the baby and sighed. It seemed as if she wanted to say something to Ch'ilsŏng, but kept fretfully caressing the baby, who looked like a sick cat.

She had weeded all day and at night had gone up to the mountain and gathered wood. Although she was dead tired, she had to look after the baby at night. Every night she felt she wouldn't be able to wake up again once she fell asleep. Ch'ilsŏng hated his mother for not looking after herself.

"Go to sleep, you chicken!" Ch'ilsŏng shouted. Yong-ae began to cry.

"How can she go to sleep? She's sick and she's starved all day and my milk's dried up," his mother wanted to say, but swallowed the words. Tears gathered in her eyes.

"Oh, it's all right. He wasn't talking to you. Suck your milk." She finished the words with difficulty. Tears streamed down her cheeks. She wished she could quench Yong-ae's thirst with her tears.

At long last his mother said, "Why would a baby get born, nearly killing its mother, if it didn't mean

보아도 무심했건만, 웬일인지 이 순간엔 이러한 생각이 일었다.

한참이나 꿈쩍 않고 있던 그는 손을 가만히 들어보고 이번에나 하는 마음이 가슴에서 후닥닥거렸다. 하나 손은 여전히 떨리어 옴츠러든다. 갑자기 윽 하고 구역질을 하자 땅에 머리를 쾅! 드쫓고 훌쩍훌쩍 울었다.

아주 캄캄해서야 어머니는 돌아왔다. 또 산으로 가서 나무를 해 이고 온 것이다.

"어디 아프냐?"

어둠 속에 약간 드러나는 어머니의 윤곽은 피로에 쌓여 넘어질 듯했다. 그리고 짙은 풀내가 치마폭에 흠씬 배어 마늘내같이 강하게 풍겼다.

"이애야, 왜 대답이 없어."

아들의 몸을 어루만지는 장작개비 같은 그 손에도 온기만은 돌았다.

칠성이는 어머니의 손을 뿌리치고 돌아누웠다. 어머니는 물러앉아 아들의 눈치를 살피다가 혼자 하는 말처럼,

"어디가 아픈 모양인데, 말을 해야지 잡놈 같으니라구."

to live? When I looked in next door just now the baby was dead. That's better for everybody, but... Oh, poor things. She had writhed so in the furrow that the baby's head was all matted with earth, I heard. If it had lived it would have become nothing but a cripple. I heard that earth went into its eyes and ears, too. Oh, it did well to die," his mother murmured fretfully. Ch'ilsŏng breathed hard because of the oppression in his chest. Then he thought he would not have had to be like this if he had died as a baby.

"Oh, what's so good about living that we have to keep alive? Kŭnnyŏn's mother said she'll go weeding again tomorrow. She needs to rest at least one day, but this is no time for resting. Oh, why do babies get born to poor folks like us?"

She recalled the time she had threshed barley the very next day after she had given birth to Yong-ae. The sky had swirled and looked yellow, and the ears of barley became in turn big balls and tiny dots. Whenever she lifted or brought down the flail something kept sinking down from her body. Later on she felt something heavy hanging between her legs, but she could not take a look at it or do anything about it, afraid that others might notice.

이 말을 남기고 일어서 나갔다. 한참 후에 어머니는 푸성귀 국에다 밥을 말아 가지고 들어와서 아들을 일으켰다. 칠성이는 언제나처럼 어머니 팔목에서 뚝 하는 소리를 들으면서 일어 앉아 떨리는 손으로 술을 붙들었다.

"이애야, 어디 아프냐?"

아까와 달리 어머니 옷가에 그을음내가 풍기고 숨소리에 따라 밥내구수한데 무겁던 몸이 가벼워진다.

"아 아니."

맘을 졸이던 끝에 비로소 안심하고 아들이 국 마시는 것을 들여다보았다.

"에그 큰년네 어머니는 오늘 밭에서 애기를 낳았다누나. 내남 없이 가난한 것들에서 새끼가 무어겠니?"

아까 버드나무 아래서 본 큰년의 어머니가 떠오르고 "으아으아" 울던 아기 울음소리가 들리는 듯, 또 영애의 그 꼴이 선히 나타난다. 그는 눈살을 찌푸렸다.

"글쎄, 새끼가 왜 태여, 진절머리 나지."

한숨 섞어 어머니는 이렇게 탄식하고, 빈 그릇을 들고 나가버린다. 칠성이는 방 안이 덥기도 하지만, 큰년네 일이 궁금해서 그만 일어나 나왔다.

When at last she looked at it in the privy, a lump of flesh as big as her fist was hanging down from her inside and blood was all over her thighs. She was frightened but too ashamed to consult anybody about it, so she left it as it was. The flesh still hung between her thighs and oozed.

Because of that she was hotter in the summer, and she stank. In the winter it was worse; she ached all over and felt chills as with an ague. If she walked far, the lump burned as if on fire and it also got so inflamed and swollen that she couldn't walk. Swellings erupted all over it, and as they festered and burst they pained her beyond description. But it was a pain she could not even talk about to anybody.

The mother sighed, thinking of the flesh hanging down damply even now. The dried leaves rustled. Yong-ae bit her mother's nipple.

"Ouch!" she cried out, but fearing that Ch'ilsŏng would swear at the baby if he knew, swallowed her next words and pressed Yong-ae's head to let her know it hurt. But, fearing again that she had pressed it too hard, she caressed the baby's head.

"Oh, in the midst of that bustle they had guests come to visit them, but the guests had to leave

뜰 한 모퉁이에 쌓여 있는 나뭇단에서 짙은 풀내가 산속인 듯싶게 흘러나오고, 검푸른 하늘의 별들은 아기 눈같이 예쁘다.

왱왱거리는 모기를 쫓으면서 나무 말려 모아놓은 곳에 주저앉았다. 마른 갈잎이 버석버석 소리를 내고 더운 김에 밑이 뜨뜻하였다. 어머니가 저리로부터 온다.

"칠성이냐? 왜 나왔니."

버석 소리를 내고 곁에 앉는다. 땀내와 영애의 똥내가 훅 끼치므로 그는 머리를 돌리었다. 어머니는 젖을 꺼내 아기에게 물리고 한숨을 푹 쉰다. 무슨 말을 하려나 하고 칠성이는 어머니의 눈치를 살피나, 안타깝게 병든 고양이 새끼 같은 영애를 어루만지기만 하고, 쉽사리 입을 열지 않았다.

해종일 김매기에 그 몸이 고달팠겠고, 더구나 산에 가서 나무를 해 오려기에 그 몸이 지칠 대로 지쳤으련만, 또 아기에게서라도 시달림을 받으니, 오늘날이라도 잠만 들면 깨지 못할 것 같다. 그렇게 피로한 몸을 돌아보지 않는 어머니가 어딘지 모르게 미웠다.

"계 계집애는 자지도 않아!"

without going in."

Ch'ilsŏng raised his head. The fragrant smell of mugwort burnt for the mosquito fire wafted over them.

"The people who'd been thinking of taking Kŭnnyŏn had come to take a look at her. Maybe you don't know about them. The man runs some sort of business in the town. I heard that he has some money. But he hasn't got a son yet. So he has taken in about a dozen women up till now, but still hasn't got a child. Oh, babies have to get born in houses like that."

His mother looked down at Yong-ae. Ch'ilsŏng didn't like to see his mother minding the baby even while talking. But he sat still waiting for her next words.

"So somebody talked to him about Kŭnnyŏn and the man said never. I heard it's because he felt sorry for his wife, but he came to take a look at her today. Why today, of all days? Maybe that's a sign Kŭnnyŏn will have luck. And she deserves it too. She's gentle and she can do any kind of work better than people who can see. Well, she'll get married into an heirless family and she'll bear a big healthy son. She has to live a better life."

칠성이는 보다 못해서 꽥 소리쳤다. 영애는 젖꼭지를 문 채 울음을 내쳤다. 그 애가 어디 자게 되었니. 몸이 아픈데다 해종일 굶었고, 또 이리 젖이 안 나니까, 하는 말이 혀끝에서 똑 떨어지려는 것을 꾹 참으니 눈물이 핑그르르 돌았다.

"오오, 널 보고 안 그런다. 어서 머."

겨우 말을 마치자, 눈물이 줄줄 흘렀다. 문득 어머니는 이 눈물이 젖으로 흘러서 영애의 타는 목을 축여줬으면 가슴은 이다지도 쓰리지 않으련만 하였다.

한참 후에 어머니는,

"글쎄 살지도 못할 것이 왜 태어나서 어미만 죽을 경을 치게 하겠니. 이제 가보니 큰년네 아기는 죽었더구나. 잘되기는 했더라만…… 에그 불쌍하지. 얼마나 밭고랑을 타고 헤매이었는지 아기 머리는 그냥 흙투성이라더구나. 그게 살면 또 병신이나 되지 뭘 하겠니. 눈에 귀에 흙이 잔뜩 들었더라니, 아이구 죽기를 잘했지, 잘했지!"

어머니는 흥분이 되어 이렇게 중얼거린다. 칠성이도 가슴이 답답해서 숨을 크게 쉬었다. 그리고 자신도 어

"What would anybody want to take a blind girl like that for!" Ch'ilsŏng yelled abruptly. He was now all aflame with jealousy, and he resolved that if anybody tried to take Kŭnnyŏn away he would fight him till death. That made him hot in the head and shaky in all four limbs.

"So, is she going to be married?"

His mother looked at her son and found it difficult to answer. When she reflected that Ch'ilsŏng was already old enough to yearn for girls, she felt sad and anxious about his future.

"It's not quite settled yet."

Ch'ilsŏng calmed down a little at that, but he felt sad and got up.

"Go in and sleep. And go to town tomorrow. We can't manage otherwise."

Ch'ilsŏng got angry and left his mother, to walk around aimlessly. As he walked he left behind the odor of mugwort, but the smell of grass floated on the crisp, cool air. Along the wind came the sound of grain stalks rubbing against each other, and the cool, light breeze hugged him softly. His pants became wet with dew and the sound of insects undulated this way and that as if he were kicking at them with his toes.

려서 죽었더라면 이 모양은 되지 않을 것을 하였다.

"사는 게 뭔지, 큰년네 어머니는 내일 또 김매러 가겠다더구나, 하루쯤 쉬어야 할 텐데, 이게 이게 어느 때냐, 그럴 처지가 되어야지, 없는 놈에게 글쎄 자식이 뭐냐, 웬 자식이냐."

영애를 낳아 놓고 그 다음 날로 보리마당질하던, 그 지긋지긋하던 때가 떠오른다. 하늘이 노랗고, 핑핑 돌고, 보리 이삭이 작았다 커 보이고, 도리깨를 들 때, 내릴 때, 아래서는 무엇이 뭉클뭉클 나오다가 나중엔 무엇이 묵직하게 매어달리는 듯해서 좀 만져보려 했으나, 사이도 없고 또 남들이 볼까 꺼리어 그냥 참고 있다가 소변보면서 보니 허벅다리엔 피가 흥건했고 또 주먹 같은 살덩이가 축 늘어져 있었다. 겁이 더럭 났지만 누구 보고 물어보기도 부끄럽고 해서 그냥 내버려 두었더니, 그 살덩이가 오늘까지 늘어져서 들어갈 줄 모르고 또 무슨 물을 줄줄 흘리고 있다.

그것 때문에 여름에는 더 덥고 또 고약스런 악취가 나고, 겨울엔 더 춥고 항상 몸살이 오는 듯 오삭오삭 추웠다. 먼 길이나 걸으면 그 살덩이가 불이 붙는 듯 쓰라

He stood still. Before him, all was hidden under cover of the opaque darkness, and only the outline of the burnt mountain stood like a heap of clouds under the sky. Over the mountain stars shone as if in competition. When starlight ling'ered on his eyes, tears gushed down and he felt like crying his heart out. The mountain and the sky all looked so unfeeling to him.

"Let's go in, dear." His mother's weak voice reached him.

"Why do you follow me around all the time?" All the resentment that had been suppressed in his heart threatened to burst out at once.

"Please, let's go in. Don't walk around like this." His mother held his hand. Ch'ilsŏng tried to shake her hand off, but he lacked strength. His mother begged, half-crying. Walking back with his mother, Ch'ilsŏng decided to see Kŭnnyŏn the next day and ask her if she was going to get married, and also if she would marry him. When he had resolved thus, his heart beat fast and he seemed to behold before him a ray of hope.

"Please have pity on me and your younger brother and sister." His mother tried to soothe him by any means. Ch'ilsŏng walked home in silence.

리고 또 염증을 일으켜 퉁퉁 부어서 걸음 걸을 수가 없으며 나중엔 주위로 수없는 종기가 나서 그것이 곪아터지느라 기막히게 아팠다. 이리 아파도 누구에게 아프다는 말도 할 수 없는 그런 종류의 병이었다.

어머니는 지금도 척척히 늘어져 있는 그 살덩이를 느끼면서 한숨을 푹 쉬었다. 갈잎이 바삭바삭 소리를 낸다. 마침 영애는 젖꼭지를 깍 깨물었다. "아이그!" 소리까지 내치고도 얼른 칠성이가 이런 줄을 알면 욕할 것이 싫어서 그 다음 말은 뚝 그치고 손으로 영애의 머리를 꾹 눌러 아프다는 뜻을 영애에게만 알리었다. 그러고도 너무 눌렀는가 하여 누른 자리를 금시로 어루만져 주었다.

"정말 오늘 그 난시에 글쎄 큰년네 집에는 손님이 와서 방 안에 앉아도 못 보고 갔다누나."

칠성이는 머리를 들었다. 어디서 불려오는 모기 쑥내는 향긋하였다.

"전에부터 말 있던 그 집에서 왔다는데 넌 정 모르기 쉽겠구나, 읍에서 무슨 장사를 한다나. 꽤 돈푼이나 있다더라. 한데, 손을 이때까지 못 보았누나, 해서, 첩을

Ch'ilsŏng got up late the next day and decided again that he would have an answer from Kŭnnyŏn that day. "What if she is already pledged in marriage?" The thought made him faint. He came out into the backyard and stood beside the hedge. All was silence inside Kŭnnyŏn's house; only the buzzing of flies around the dirty water basin could be heard. "I won't let her!" He stepped away from the hedge at once. The white stones in front of him looked yellow for some reason.

He went into the room panting. He looked at himself and thought, "I can't go to meet her like this!" There were traces of cowdung on his clothes and they were also torn here and there. But he quickly reminded himself that Kŭnnyŏn couldn't see, and tried to figure out what to say to her, looking up at the ceiling. He swallowed many times, but he could not think of a word to say. He felt as if he had never known how to speak in all his life.

Suddenly he felt weak when it crossed his mind that she might already know he was a cripple. He looked outside dispiritedly as he imagined Kŭnnyŏn saying, "Who would marry someone like you?"

여남은두 넘어 얻었으나 이때까지 못 낳았단다. 에그 그런 집에나 태이지."

어머니는 영애를 잠잠히 내려다본다. 칠성이는 이야기하면서도 아기를 생각하는 어머니가 보기 싫었다. 하나 다음 말을 들으려니 가만히 앉아 있었다.

"그런데 어찌어찌하다가 큰년의 말이 났는데 사내는 펄쩍 뛰더란다. 그래두 안으로 맘이 켕기어서 그러하다고 하더니, 하필 오늘 같은 날, 글쎄 선보러 왔다 갔다니…… 큰년이는 이제 복 좋을라! 언제 봐도 덕성스러워. 그 애가 눈이 멀었다 뿐이지 못 하는 게 뭐 있어야지. 허드렛일이나 앉아 하는 일이나 휑 잡았으니 눈 뜬 사람보다 낫다. 이제 그런 집으로 시집가게 되고 달덩이 같은 아들을 낳아 놀게다. 아이그, 좀 잘 살아야지……."

"눈 눈 먼 것을 얻어야 뭘 뭘을 해!"

칠성이는 뜻밖에 이런 말을 퉁명스레 내친다. 그의 가슴은 지금 질투의 불길로 꽉 찼고, 누구든지 큰년이만 다친다면 사생을 결단하리라 하였다. 이러고 나니 머리에 열이 오르고 다리팔이 풀풀 떨리었다.

The leaves of the squash and the gourd vines that wound around the hedge, of the corn stalks and apricot trees and the bush clover that stretched upward toward the sky, all shook freely and blithely in the breeze. He felt somehow less free than those plants and trees, and he sighed till his whole body shook.

At last Ch'ilsŏng emerged from his yard with firm resolution and, after pacing in front of Kŭnnyŏn's house several times, pushed open the bush clover gate and strode in.

The door to the dirt-floored room was shut, and only a bush clover broom lay in the yard. When he opened the door a cat jumped out, mewing. He was so frightened that his heart throbbed wildly. He stepped on to the dirt floor and after much hesitation opened the door of the inner room. Only heavy air moved out toward him; Kŭnnyŏn was not there. He suspected at once that she had gotten married already, and searched the kitchen and the backyard. As he was about to give up and turn back, he heard the bush clover gate open. Frightened, he ran to a post and stepped close to the straw mat stored behind it. The door of the kitchen opened noisily and Kŭnnyŏn came in with the

"그 그래, 시 시집가기로 됐나?"

어머니는 아들의 눈치를 살피고 어쩐지 대답하기가 어려웠다. 동시에 저것도 계집이 그리우려니 하니 불쌍한 마음이 들고 또 아들의 장래가 캄캄해 보이었다.

"아직은 되지 않았다더라만은……."

이 말에 그의 맘은 다소 가라앉은 듯하나, 웬일인지 슬픈 생각이 들어 그는 일어났다.

"들어가 자거라, 내일은 일찍이 읍에 가게 해. 어떡허겠니?"

칠성이는 화를 버럭 내고 어머니 곁을 떠나 되는 대로 걸었다.

발걸음에 따라 모기쑥내 없어지고 산뜻한 공기 속에 풀내 가득히 흐른다. 멀리 곡식대 비벼치는 소리 바람결에 은은하고, 산기를 띤 실바람이 그의 몸에 싸물싸물 기고 있다. 잠방이 가랑이 이슬에 젖고, 벌레 소리 발끝에 채어 요리 졸졸졸, 조리 쓸쓸쓸…….

그는 우뚝 섰다. 저 앞은 지척을 분간할 수 없는 어둠으로 덮였고, 하늘 아래 저 불타산의 윤곽만이 검은 구름같이 뭉실뭉실 떠 있다. 그 위에 별들이 너도나도 빛

wooden laundry basin. He felt faint and weak. He felt as if Kŭnnyŏn could see and would come up to him; as if she was not blind, but could always open her eyelids and see with her starry eyes. Feeling he was about to suffocate any moment, he suppressed his breath and went behind the straw mat. But his breath came in wilder pants, and he felt as if the straw mat would block his nostrils and make him swoon.

Kŭnnyŏn went out into the backyard. Hearing the dragging of her shoes, he stuck out his head, peered about, and tried to move his feet; but his whole body twitched convulsively and he could not move a step. He thought of giving up and going home. He felt as if his body had been made of stone. But then the hedge rustled as Kŭnnyŏn spread laundry on it and he remembered "Kŭnnyŏn is going to marry a man in town!" His feet began to move in wild staggering.

Kŭnnyŏn, in the middle of spreading a piece of laundry on the hedge, sharply turned her face and halted. Ch'ilsŏng dared not look at Kŭnnyŏn but stood there like one out of his wits.

"Who is it?"

Silence.

나고, 별빛이 눈가에 흐르자 눈물이 핑그르르 돌며 통곡이라도 하고 싶었다. 저 산도 저 하늘도 너무나 그에겐 무심한 것 같다.

"이애야, 들어가자."

어머니의 기운 없는 음성이 들린다.

"왜 왜 쫓아 다 다녀유."

칠성의 마음에 잠겼던 어떤 원한이 일시에 머리를 들려고 하였다.

"제발 들어가. 이리 나오면 어쩌겠니."

어머니는 그의 손을 붙들었다. 칠성이는 뿌리치려 했으나 힘이 부친다. 긴 풀이 그들의 옷에 비비쳐 실실 소리를 낸다. 어머니는 절반 울면서 사정을 하였다. 그는 어머니 손에 붙들리어 돌아오면서, 오냐 내일 저를 만나보고 시집가는지 안 가는지 물어보고, 또 나한테 시집오겠니도 물어야지 할 때 가슴은 씩씩 뛰고 어떤 실 같은 희망이 보인다.

"날 보고 네 동생들을 봐라."

어머니는 이러한 말을 하여 아들을 달래려고 한다. 칠성이는 말없이 그의 집까지 왔다.

"Who is it?" Kŭnnyŏn's voice was shaky. Ch'ilsŏng thought he had to say something, anything, but his lips refused to move. At long last he moved forward one step.

"Oh, it's you." Kŭnnyŏn moved close to the hedge and bowed her head. Her softly closed eyelids were tremulous. Ch'ilsŏng became a little bolder as Kŭnnyŏn recognized him. He began to worry about the outside now, and he kept looking out.

"Go away! My mother will be back soon." Kŭnnyŏn spoke decisively. Her voice was the same as when she was a child.

"I heard you're going to get married. You must be happy."

"What foolish talk. Go away!" Kŭnnyŏn, fingering her laundry, sighed softly. White flesh peeped from between the rents in her thin blouse. Ch'ilsŏng stepped close to her unawares.

"Oh, Mother!" Kŭnnyŏn shouted, grasping the hedge. Ch'ilsŏng became fearful and thought of retreating. He felt faint and the ground swirled before him.

"My mother's coming."

Ch'ilsŏng opened his eyes at the sound of Kŭnnyŏn's trembling voice. The thick braid of

이튿날 일부러 늦게 일어난 칠성이는 오늘은 기어코 큰년이를 만나 무슨 말이든지 하리라, 만일 시집가기로 되었다면…… 그는 아뜩하였다. 그때는 그만 죽여 버릴까, 나두 그 칼에 죽지 하고 뒤뜰로 나와서 바자 곁에 다가섰다. 큰년네 집은 고요하고 뜨물동이에서 왕왕거리는 파리 소리만이 간혹 들릴 뿐이다. 가자! 바자에서 선뜻 물러섰다. 눈에 마주 띄는 저 앞의 큰 차돌은 웬일인지 노랗게 보이었다.

그는 숨이 차서 방으로 들어왔다. 옷을 이 모양을 하구 가, 하고 굽어보았다. 쇠똥자국이 여기저기 있고, 군데군데 해졌고, 뭘 눈이 멀었는데 이게 보이나, 그럼 만나서는 뭐라구 말을 해야지, 그는 천정을 바라보고 생각하였다. 입가에 흐르는 침을 몇 번이나 시 하고 들여마시나 그저 캄캄한 것뿐이다. 생전 말이라고는 못 해 본 것처럼 아뜩하였다.

내가 병신임을 제가 아나, 하는 불안이 불쑥 일어 맥이 탁 풀린다. "너까짓 것에게 시집 가!" 하는 큰년의 말이 들리는 듯해서 그는 시름없이 밖을 내다보았다.

바자에 얽힌 호박넝쿨, 박넝쿨, 그 옆으로 옥수숫대,

glossy black hair on her back smelt intensely of Kŭnnyŏn. Ch'ilsŏng pressed Kŭnnyŏn's foot with his foot. Kŭnnyŏn blushed and, withdrawing her foot, moved away. The laundry in her hand fell limply to the ground.

Ch'ilsŏng feared that she might pick up a stone and hit him, but Kŭnnyŏn stepped close to the hedge and just fingered the bush clover twigs. Her hair ribbon blew in the breeze. She did not say another word, but just fingered the twigs of the hedge.

"I'll give you sweets and... and clothes, too. You won't get married, will you, if I do?"

Kŭnnyŏn kept silent for a long time and then, raising her head a little, said, "Who cares for sweets?" and laughed softly.

Ch'ilsŏng also laughed and asked again, "You won't, will you?"

"How do I know? My father knows."

Ch'ilsŏng was at a loss for words at that. So he just stood there like a fool.

"Get out at once." Kŭnnyŏn turned her face toward him. She had thick eyelashes over softly closed eyes, and hanging at the tips of her eyelashes were drops of anxiety.

썩 나와서 살구나무, 작고 큰 댑싸리가 아무 기탄없이 하늘을 바라보고 가지가지를 쭉쭉 쳤으며 잎잎이 자유스럽게 미풍에 흔들리지 않는가. 웬일인지 자신은 저러한 초목만큼도 자유롭지 못한 것을 전신에 느끼고 한숨을 후 쉬었다.

한참 후에 칠성이는 마음을 단단히 먹고 마당으로 나와서 큰년네 집 앞으로 몇 번이나 왔다 갔다 하다가 사리문을 가만히 밀고 껑충 뛰어들었다.

봉당문도 꼭 닫히었고 싸리비만이 한가롭게 놓여 있다. 얼떨결에 봉당문을 삐걱 열었을 때 고양이 한 마리가 야옹 하고 튀어나간다. 그는 어찌 놀랐는지 숨이 하늘에 닿을 것처럼 뛰었다. 봉당으로 들어서서 한참이나 망설이다가 방문을 열어보았다. 무거운 공기만이 밀려나오고 큰년이는 없었다. 시집을 갔나? 하고 얼른 생각하면서, 부엌으로 뒤뜰로 인기척을 찾으려 하였으나 조용하였다. 그는 이러하고 언제까지나 있을 수가 없어서 발길을 돌리려 했을 때 싸리문 소리가 난다. 그는 얼떨결에 기둥 이편으로 와서 그 뒤 멍석 곁에 바싹 다가섰다. 부엌문 소리가 덜거렁 나더니 큰년이가 빨래 함지

"Well, are you going to get married, then?"

Kŭnnyŏn dropped her head and rolled a stone with the tip of her shoe. Ch'ilsŏng felt like crying.

"You won't? Promise?"

Kŭnnyŏn, instead of answering, sighed and turned away. The baby cried just then. Ch'ilsŏng, startled, ran out.

When he got home, he saw Ch'il-un tying the baby with a strip of cloth. She was rolling on the floor of the kitchen. The baby moved her thin limbs wildly and struggled. Ch'il-un hit her as if she had been a dead fish.

"Are you going to sleep or not? If you won't sleep, then I'll kill you." He waved a fist at the baby, his nose dripping from both nostrils. The baby shook like a leaf and tears kept flowing out of her closed eyes.

"Yes! Close your eyes like that and sleep!" Ch'il-un lay down beside the baby and squeezed his side with one hand.

"Mother, it hurts here so much, I can't carry the baby any more. I can't," Ch'il-un murmured, snuffling. Presently, drowsiness filled his eyes and he fell asleep. Ch'ilsŏng looked down at his brother absently and stepped onto the dirt floor.

를 이고 들어온다. 그의 눈은 캄캄해지고 전신이 나른해진다. 큰년이가 그를 알아보고 이리 오는 것만 같고, 그의 눈은 먼 것이 아니고 언제나 창틈으로 볼 수 있는 별 눈을 빠끔히 뜨고서 쳐다보는 듯했다. 숨이 차서 견딜 수 없으므로 멍석 아래 뒤로 돌아가며 숨을 죽이었으나 점점 더 숨결이 항항거리고 멍석눈에 코가 맞닿아서 기절을 할 지경이었다.

큰년이는 뒤뜰로 나간다. 짤짤 끄는 신발 소리를 들으면서 머리를 내밀어 밖을 살피고 발길을 옮기려 했으나 온몸이 비비 꼬이어 한 보를 옮길 수가 없다. 어색하여 그만 집으로 가려고도 했다. 그의 몸은 돌로 된 것 같았으나 마침 빨래 널리는 소리가 바삭바삭 나자 큰년이가 읍으로 시집간다 하는 생각이 들며 발길이 허둥하고 떨어진다.

큰년이는 빨래를 바자에 걸치다가 휘끈 돌아보고 주춤한다. 칠성이는 차마 큰년이를 쳐다보지 못하고 우두커니 서 있었다.

"누구요?"

"……."

"Mama!" The baby he thought was sleeping opened her round eyes and looked up at her brother. Ch'ilsŏng got frightened. Unconsciously he lifted a foot and raised an eyebrow, as if to kick her. The baby twisted her thin lips and closed her eyes.

"Mama! Mama!" the baby's mouth was calling and tears were running down her cheeks. Ch'ilsŏng went into the room, paced it in a circle a few times and came out into the backyard. Hoping Kŭnnyŏn was still standing in her yard, he carefully parted the brushwood of the hedge and peeped in. Kŭnnyŏn was not there; only the laundered clothes lay spread over the hedge.

He came into the room and, looking up at the beggar's sack hanging on the wall, thought about how he would buy material for Kŭnnyŏn's clothes. He thought to himself, who knows but that might show his heart to Kŭnnyŏn and her parents, too? He slung his sack over his shoulder sideways and, putting the straw hat on his head, went outside. Passing the kitchen, he caught sight of the baby lapping up something. When he looked around he saw that the baby was drinking her own urine beside the stove.

"누구야요?"

큰년의 음성은 떨려 나왔다. 칠성이는 무슨 말이든지 해야 할 터인데 입이 깍 붙고 떨어지지 않는다. 한참 후에 발길을 지척하고 내디디었다.

"난 누구라구……."

큰년이는 바자 곁으로 다가서고 머리를 다소곳 한다. 곱게 감은 그의 눈등은 발랑발랑 떨렸다. 칠성이는 자기를 알아보는 것을 알고 조금 마음이 대담해졌다. 이번엔 밖이 걱정이 되어 연신 눈이 그리로만 간다.

"나가야, 어머니 오신다."

큰년이는 암팡지게 말을 했다. 어려서 음성이 그대로 남아 있다.

"너 너 시집간다지. 좋겠구나!"

"새끼두 별소리 다하네. 나가야."

큰년이는 빨래를 조물락거리고 서서 숨을 가볍게 쉰다. 해어진 적삼등에 흰 살이 불룩 솟아 있다. 칠성이는 무의식간에 다가섰다.

"아이구머니!"

큰년이는 바자를 붙들고 소리쳤다. 칠성이는 와락 겁

"You! Dirty thing!" Ch'ilsŏng growled and went out to the street. It was hot, as if he had stepped into hot water. Taking the new highway, he arranged his clothes and hat and tried to walk with dignity. He thought he would have to look more like a gentleman from now on. He coughed a solemn false cough and tried to walk slowly. Well, if he walked like that the children wouldn't pester him or the grown-ups make fun of him. He recalled Kŭnnyŏn's face as he had this thought. He looked back stealthily, but his village was already out of sight and only the Indian millet field filled his view. As he walked near the field the smell of young Indian millet leaves floated past and sweat ran down his back. He jerked his body once or twice and looked in no particular direction.

The burnt mountain that shone green beyond the Indian millet field looked so close that it seemed he could reach its top if he moved only a few steps. It was the same mountain that he could see at leisure from the window of his house, and it was also the mountain that he could look at while trying to walk inconspicuously past an Indian millet field like this.

He exhaled a deep sigh. Whenever he looked at the mountain he felt his torn mind compose itself,

이 일어 주춤 물러서고 나갈까도 했다. 앞이 캄캄해지고 또 빙글빙글 돌아가는 것 같았다.

"어머니 오신다야."

칠성이는 잠깐 눈을 감았다가 덜덜 떨리어 나오는 이 소리에 눈을 떴다. 등어리로 흘러내려온 삼단 같은 머리채는 큰년의 냄새를 물씬물씬 피우고 있다. 칠성이는 얼른 큰년의 발을 짐짓 밟았다. 큰년이는 얼굴이 새빨개서 발을 냉큼 빼어 가지고 저리로 간다. 손에 들었던 빨래는 맥없이 툭 떨어진다.

재가 돌을 집어 치려고 저러나 하고 겁을 먹었으나, 큰년이는 바자 곁에 다가서서 바자를 보시락보시락 만지고 있는데, 댕기꼬리를 풀풀 떨린다. 야물야물 하던 말도 쑥 들어가고 애꿎은 바자만 만지고 있다.

"사탕두 주구, 옷 옷감두 주 주께, 시집 안 가지?"

큰년이는 언제까지나 잠잠하고 있다가, 조금 머리를 드는 척하더니,

"누가…… 사탕…… 히."

속으로 웃는다. 칠성이도 따라 웃고,

"응 야 안 안 가지?"

and recalled things from his childhood he had quite forgotten.

One spring day when mist was rising from the distant mountain, he woke up in the morning and from his window he saw his friends going up the mountain in single file with A-frame racks on their backs and long staffs stuck sideways across their A-frames. He envied them so much that he sighed and looked at them like a mindless boy, thinking, when will I be all right again and able to go up the mountain to gather wood like those boys, with a staff stuck in the A-frame slung over my back? And he thought that when he grew up he would climb the mountain and split thick boughs and bring down more wood than the A-frame could hold.

He sneered at himself when he recalled that thought. All the joints in his bones ached, and his heart contracted. He shook his head a couple of times and trudged on. Before his eyes was only Kŭnnyŏn now.

Two days later.

Ch'ilsŏng was standing at the entrance of the town of Songhwa, six miles from his village. He could not earn much by begging in the town near his village, so he had roamed on to Songhwa. After

"내가 아니, 아버지가 알지."

이 말엔 말이 막힌다. 그래서 우두커니 섰노라니,

"어서 나가 야."

큰년이는 얼굴을 돌린다. 곱게 감은 눈에 속눈썹이 가무레하게 났는데 그 눈썹 끝에 걱정이 대글대글 맺혀 있다.

"그 그럼 시집 가 가겠니?"

큰년이는 머리를 푹 숙이고, 발끝으로 돌을 굴리고 있다. 칠성이는 슬픈 맘이 들어 울고 싶었다.

"안 안 안 가지, 응야?"

큰년이는 대답 대신으로 한숨을 푹 쉬고 머리를 들려다가 돌아선다. 그때 어린애 울음소리가 들렸다. 칠성이는 놀라 뛰어나왔다.

집에 오니, 칠운이가 아기를 부엌 바닥에 내려 굴리고 띠로 아기를 꽁꽁 동이려고 한다. 아기는 다리팔을 함부로 놀리고 발악을 하니, 칠운이는 사뭇 죽일 고기를 다루듯 아기를 칵칵 쥐어박는다.

"이 계집애 자겠니 안 자겠니. 안 자면 죽이고 말겠다."

시퍼런 코를 쌍줄로 흘리고서 주먹을 겨누어 보인다.

two days and nights of begging he at last managed to buy some cotton material for Kŭnnyŏn's dress and was going back home.

He thought of spending that night somewhere, but decided to start for home at once because he wanted to give the gift to Kŭnnyŏn quickly, and also because he was worried about Kŭnnyŏn's rumored marriage.

The starless sky and the furry-soft darkness dazed his eyes, but for some reason his mind was at rest, and a certain degree of hope brightened his eyes. He could distinctly discern the mountains and the waters, as if they lived in his mind's eye, and even the pebbles on the highway seemed to be amicably inviting him to play with them.

He thought he liked the road at night much more than in the daytime, when cars ran past raising dust and endless pedestrians walked on it. So he walked on, without feeling any pain in his legs. When he halted his steps, the smell of the mountain welcomed him and the running brook whispered to him. The smell of mud also wafted up to him from the rice paddy, and when mountain birds resumed singing, the distant glow of lamps seemed to float up and fly away.

아기는 바르르 떨면서 눈을 꼭 감고 눈물을 졸졸 흘리고 있다.

“그러구 자라. 이 계집애.”

칠운이는 아기 옆에 엎어지고 한 손으로 그의 허리를 꼬집어 당긴다.

“어마이, 난 여기 자꾸자꾸 아파서 아기 못 보겠다야 씨…… 흥.”

코를 혀끝으로 빨아올리면서 칠운이는 이렇게 중얼거렸다. 그 눈에 졸음이 가득하더니 그만 씩씩 자버린다.

칠성이는 무심히 이 꼴을 보고 봉당으로 들어섰다.

“엄마!”

자는 줄 알았던 아기가 눈을 동글하게 뜨고 오빠를 바라본다. 칠성이는 머리끝이 쭈뼛하도록 놀랐다. 해서 얼결에 발을 이어 찰 것처럼 하고 눈을 딱 부릅떠 보이니 아기는 그 얇은 입술을 비죽비죽하며 눈을 감는다.

“엄마! 엄마!”

아기는 그 입으로 이렇게 부르고 울었다. 칠성이는 방으로 들어와서 빙빙 돌다가 뒤뜰로 나와 큰년이가 아직도 그 자리에 서 있으면 하고 바자를 가만히 빼개고 들

Every time he breathed, the fabric for Kŭnnyŏn's clothes touched his chest like the skin of a girl and made his flesh thrill down to the toes. "How shall I give it to her?" He opened his mouth unconsciously and made as if to mouth something. He pictured himself standing face to face with Kŭnnyŏn. "When I give her this cloth, Kŭnnyŏn will blossom with smiles to the tips of her thick eyelashes!" His heart pumped noisily.

Raindrops began to fall as dawn broke in the eastern sky. He became frightened and started to run, but the rain came thicker and the wind scattered it with a sound like the fluttering of a flock of sparrows.

He hesitated over what to do for a while, and turned his steps toward a village that showed its dim outline through the thick screen of rain. If it hadn't been for Kŭnnyŏn's cloth he would have marched on, rain or no rain, but he feared that the precious fabric would get wet from the rain, so he decided to seek shelter in the nearby village.

When he looked back after walking a good while the highway could be seen distinctly, and for some reason he felt unwilling to move, but he forced himself on.

여다보니 큰년이는 보이지 않고 빨래만이 가득히 널려 있었다.

방으로 들어와서 벽에 걸린 동냥자루를 한참이나 바라보면서 큰년의 옷감 끊어다 줄 궁량을 하고, 그러면 큰년이와 그의 부모들도 나에게로 뜻이 옮겨질지 누가 아나 하고, 동냥자루를 벗겨 메구서 밀짚모를 비스듬히 제껴 쓴 다음에 방문을 나섰다. 눈결에 보니 아기는 무엇을 먹고 있으므로, 그는 머리를 넘석하여 보았다. 아기는 띠 동인 데서 벗어나와 아궁 곁에 오줌을 눈 듯한데 그 오줌을 쪽쪽 핥아먹고 있다.

“이 애! 이 계집애!”

칠성이는 이렇게 버럭 소리를 지르고 밖으로 나왔다. 뜨거운 물 속에 들어서는 듯 전신이 후끈하였다. 신작로에 올라서며 그는 옷을 바로 하고 모자를 고쳐 쓰고 아주 점잖은 양 하였다. 이제부터는 이래야 할 것 같다. 에헴! 하고 큰기침도 하여 보고, 걸음도 천천히 걸으려 했다. 이러면 애들도 달려들지 못하고 어른들도 놀리지 못할 테지, 할 때 큰년이가 떠오른다. 슬며시 돌아보니, 벌써 그의 마을은 보이지 않고, 수수밭이 탁 막아섰다.

When he reached the village, smell of wet straw invaded his nostrils and as he walked past a privy the stink stung them. He stepped under the eaves of a house. He felt chilly all over and his eyes were tired so he moved next to the wall and crouched down beside it. An image of the spindly tree at the entrance of his village flitted before his eyes. Kŭnnyŏn appeared before him. He opened his eyes wide.

Day had dawned amid the rain. The distant mountain could be seen, the cluster of roofs revealed itself, and water dripped from the eaves noisily. He mustered his courage, stood up, and looked around.

He saw that the house he was standing by looked like a rich man's. The walls were of cement, and the roof was of dark, baked tiles; the wooden gate was large and studded with nails with heads as big as his fists. He felt his frozen heart thaw.

The marble nameplate looked dignified. Surrounded by the sound of raindrops, Ch'ilsŏng looked at the nameplate hard and kept on thinking.

"Maybe this is a lucky day for me. Maybe I can get a good breakfast at this house, and some rice or money too." He squeezed his eyes shut and

수수밭 곁으로 다가서니, 싱싱한 수숫잎내가 후끈 끼치고, 등허리가 근질근질하게 땀이 흘러내린다. 두어 번 몸을 움직이고 어디라 없이 바라보았다.

수수밭 머리로 파랗게 보이는 저 불타산은 몇 발걸음 옮기면 올라갈 듯이 그렇게 가까워 보인다. 그의 집 창문 곁에 비껴 서서 맘 놓고 바라볼 수 있는 것은 저 산이요, 또 이런 수수밭 머리에서 쉬어가며 바라볼 수 있는 것이 저 산이다.

그는 한숨을 푹 쉬었다. 언제나 저 산을 바라볼 때엔 흩어졌던 마음이 한데 모이는 듯하고 또한 깜박 잊었던 옛날 일이 한두 가지 생각되곤 하였다.

먼 산에 아지랑이 아물아물 기는 어느 봄날, 그는 자리에서 일어나 창문 곁에 서니, 동무들이 조그만 지게를 지고, 지팡이를 지게에 끼웃이 꽂아 가지고, 열을 지어 산으로 가고 있다. 어찌나 부럽던지 단숨에 뛰어나와서, 우두커니 바라볼 때, 언제나 나도 이 병이 나아서 재들처럼 지팡이를 저리 꽂아 가지고 나무하러 가보나. 난 어른이 되면 저 산에 가서 이런 굵은 나무를 탕탕 찍어서 한 짐 잔뜩 지고 올 테야.

thought, "Shall I pretend to be blind, too? Maybe that would make me look more pitiful and they might give me more rice and money." He tried to keep his eyes shut but his eyelids itched and his eyelashes trembled, and the marble nameplate criss-crossed his view, so that at last he opened his eyes.

"What shall I do? Maybe my clothes are too clean." He ran at once toward the muddy spot where he had been squatting. He felt even more chilly, and his lips trembled. As he was about to peep in through the crack between the two panels of the gate he heard footsteps and quickly moved aside. The gate opened with a loud squeak. As always when people looked at him, Ch'ilsŏng dropped his head and stood uneasily.

"Who is it?" It was a thick voice. Ch'ilsŏng looked up. The man had long, narrow horizontal eyes and looked like a servant, clad in black clothes.

"I... want some food."

"So early in the morning?" the man muttered to himself and turned back toward the main building.

"This is a charitable house. Other people would have tried to chase me away first." Ch'ilsŏng congratulated himself and looked in.

여기까지 생각한 그는 흠 하고 코웃음 쳤다. 뼈 마디마디가 짜릿해 오고, 가슴이 죄어지는 것 같다. 두어 번 머리를 설레설레 흔들고 터벅터벅 걸었다. 지금 그의 앞엔 큰년이가 있을 따름이다.

이틀 후.

칠성이는 그의 마을로부터 육 리나 떨어져 있는 송화읍 어구에 우두커니 서 있었다. 읍에 와서 돌아다니나 수입이 잘 되지 않으므로 이렇게 송화읍까지 오게 되었고, 그래서야 겨우 큰년의 옷감을 인조견으로 바꾸어 가지고 돌아오는 길이었던 것이다.

이 밤이나 어디서 지낼까 망설이다, 어서 빨리 이 옷감을 큰년의 손에 쥐어주고 싶은 마음, 또는 큰년의 혼사 사건이 궁금하고 불안해서 그는 가기로 결정하고 걸었다.

쳐다보니, 별도 없는 하늘, 검정 강아지 같은 어둠이 눈 속을 아물아물하게 하는데, 웬일인지 맘이 푹 놓이게 어떤 희망으로 그의 눈은 차차로 열렸다. 산과 물은 그의 맘속에 파랗게 솟아 있는 듯, 그렇게 분명히 구별할 수 있고, 신작로에 깔린 조약돌은 심심하면 장난치

The elevated building with the wooden porch attached looked like the master's study; to one side of it was a small gate, and beyond the gate the living-room floor of the inner quarters could be glimpsed. Stretching from the left of the study up to the front gate was a room that looked like a storehouse, and in front of it lay stacks of straw. Yellowish water dripped from the straw stacks. In the spacious front yard water flowed forcefully in a stream, creating a furrow.

"I'll have to go in there to get some food," he thought, and began walking awkwardly toward the inner gate. When he stepped over the threshold of the middle gate, a dog shot out from the inner kitchen like an arrow. When it growled at him, Ch'ilsŏng stepped back one step and clucked his tongue to appease it. The dog bared its sharp teeth and, jumping up, pulled at the beggar's sack with its teeth. Ch'ilsŏng shouted and ran out past the middle gate. He hoped someone was in the study to call the dog back, but no sound came from there. The dog rolled its eyes and, raising its forefeet, tried to jump up to his face. Ch'ilsŏng held his begging sack with his teeth and kept bending and stretching his body. But the dog did not abate its

기 알맞았다.

사람들이 연락부절하고, 자동차가 먼지를 피우며 달아나는 그 낮길보다는 오히려 이 밤길이 그에게는 퍽이나 좋게 생각되었다. 그래서 다리 아픈 것도 모르고 걸었다.

가다가 우뚝 서면 산냄새 그윽하고, 또 가다가 들으면 물소리 돌돌 하는데, 논물내 확 풍기고, 간혹 산새 울음 끊었다 이어질 제, 멀리 깜박여오는 동네의 등불은 포르릉 날아오는 것 같다가도 다시 보면 포르릉 날아간다.

그가 숨을 크게 쉴 때마다 가슴에 품겨 있는 큰년의 옷감은 계집의 살결 같아 조약돌을 밟는 발가락이 짜르르 울리었다.

"고것 어떡하나?"

그는 무의식 간에 입을 쩍 벌리고 무엇을 물어 당길 것처럼 하였다. 지금 큰년이와 마주 섰던 것을 머리에 그려본 것이다. 이제 가서 옷감을 들려주면 큰년이는 너무 좋아서 그 가무레한 눈썹 끝에 웃음을 띨 테지. 가슴은 소리를 내고 뛴다.

차츰 동녘 하늘이 바다와 같이 훤해 오는데 난데없는

attack, and Ch'ilsŏng had to make a further retreat. The dog followed him to the main gate and, when Ch'ilsŏng hesitated to make an exit, ran up to him and pulled at his trouser leg with its teeth. Ch'ilsŏng screamed and ran. The man came out from inside.

"C'mon, c'mon."

The dog ignored the call and kept barking with its sharp muzzle. Ch'ilsŏng looked back at the dog with murder in his eyes. The man beckoned to the dog with his hand. The dog slowly retreated with backward steps, still keeping its eyes on Ch'ilsŏng.

Ch'llsŏng suddenly felt nauseated and a chill ran down his spine. He felt feverish all at once. He looked for the dog but it was not there. Instead, the big, ugly gate blocked his view impudently. He thought of knocking on it again, but he shuddered to think of encountering the dog again. He gave up and staggered on.

The rain whipped him mercilessly, while the wind and the sounds of the trees shaking and the water flowing in the ditch almost split his eardrums. On the surface of the muddy water that flowed in swirls floated whitish straw, and leaves whirled swiftly like green birds.

The wet clothes clung to his body mercilessly

빗방울이 뚝뚝 떨어진다. 그는 놀라 자꾸 뛰었으나, 비는 더 쏟아지고, 멀리서 비 몰아오는 소리가 참새 무리들 건너 듯했다. 그는 어쩔까 잠시 망설이다가, 빗발에 묻히어 어림해 보이는 저 동리로 부득이 발길을 옮겼다. 큰년의 옷감이 아니면 이 비를 맞으면서도 가겠으나 모처럼 끊은 이 옷감이 비에 젖을 것이 안 되어 동네로 발길을 옮긴 것이다.

한참 오다가 돌아보니, 신작로가 뚜렷이 보이고 어쩐지 맘이 수선해서 발길이 딱 붙는 것을 겨우 떼어놓았다.

동네까지 오니, 비에 젖은 밀짚내 콜콜 올라오고, 변소 옆을 지나는지 거름내가 코밑에 살살 기고 있다. 그는 어떤 집 처마 아래로 들어섰다. 몸이 오솔오솔 춥고 눈이 피로해서 바싹 벽으로 다가서서 웅크리고 앉아 눈을 감았다. 그의 마을 앞에 홰나무가 보이고 큰년이가 나타나고…… 눈을 번쩍 떴다.

빗발 속에 날이 밝았는데, 먼 산이 보이고 또 지붕이 옹기종기 나타나고, 낙숫물 소리 요란하고, 그는 용기를 내어 일어나 둘러보았다.

그가 서 있는 이 집이란 돈푼이나 좋이 있는 집 같았

and the tempestuous wind made him pant for breath. He looked around, hoping to find something, but all the gates of the houses were tightly shut and breakfast smoke rose from the chimneys. He hoped to find an empty house or a water mill, but before his heavy eyes the dog kept jumping up and down, and he felt as if it were following him. The trouser leg torn by the dog flapped as he walked and disclosed his yellow, withered leg. The rain dripping from his tattered straw hat, worn low over his eyes, felt as salty on his lips as tears. He suddenly felt like crying when he thought of the material getting wet.

He stood still. The rain was so thick that he could not discern where the mountain was and where the brook, while through the madly flapping grain stalks a loud, heavy sound like a huge animal roaring shook the earth.

He ardently wished to advance, but his feet refused to move. He looked back, to note that he had almost passed the village. He moved toward the two or three houses at the end of the village, but kept gazing at the field, as if he had some unfinished business.

It was not the first time that he had been chased

다. 우선 벽이 회벽으로 되었고, 지붕은 시커먼 기와로 되었으며 널빤지로 짠 문의 규모가 크고 또 주먹 같은 못이 툭툭 박힌 것을 보아 짐작할 수 있었다. 그의 얼었던 마음이 다소 풀리는 듯하였다.

흰 돌로 된 문패가 빗소리 속에 적적한데 칠성이는 눈썹 끝이 희어지도록 이 문패를 바라보고 생각을 계속하였다. '오냐, 오늘은 내게 무슨 재수가 들어 닿나 보다. 이 집에서 조반이나 톡톡히 얻어먹고, 돈이나 쌀이나 큼직히 얻으리라…….' 얼른 눈을 꾹 감아 보고, '눈도면 체할까. 그러면 더 불쌍하게 봐서 쌀이랑 돈을 더 줄지 모르지.' 애써 눈을 감고, 한참을 견디려 했으나 눈등이 간지럽고 속눈썹이 자꾸만 떨리고 흰 문패가 가로세로 나타나고 못 견디어 눈을 뜨고 말았다.

어떡허나 내 옷이 너무 희지, 단숨에 뛰어나와서 흙물에 주저앉았다가, 일어나 섰던 자리로 왔다. 아까보다 더 춥고 입술이 떨린다. 그는 대문 틈에 눈을 대고 안을 엿보려 할 때, 신발 소리가 절벅절벅 나므로, 날래 몸을 움직이어 비껴 섰다. 대문은 요란스런 소리를 내고 열렸다. 언제나처럼 칠성이는 머리를 푹 숙이고 어떤 사

away by a dog; and countless times he had been abused and persecuted by men, too. But somehow he felt an uncontrollable fury today.

"Why are you standing there like that?"

He looked back in surprise to find that he was standing before a small building which apparently was a water-mill. The man who was looking at him with outstretched neck looked between forty and fifty, and Ch'ilsŏng could instantly tell that he was a cripple and a beggar like himself. The man grinned. He did not feel like going in, but entered after some hesitation. With a strong smell of rice husks came also the stink of horse droppings.

"Come over here. Oh, your clothes are all wet."

The man raised himself leaning on his crutches, spread the straw mat he had been sitting on, and sat down on one corner of it. Ch'ilsŏng quickly noted the man's gray hair and beard. He feared that the man might try to take away his earnings.

"You must be cold because of those wet clothes. Here, put on my old jacket and take them off and dry them." The man searched his bundle and said, "Here it is. Come on."

Ch'ilsŏng looked back. It was a dark, western jacket patched in several places. He envied the man

람의 시선을 거북스러이 느꼈다.

"웬 사람이야?"

굵직한 음성, 머리를 드니 사나이는 눈이 길게 찢어졌고, 이 집의 고용인인 듯 옷이 캄캄하다.

"한술 얻어먹으러 왔수."

"오늘은 첫새벽부터야."

사나이는 이렇게 지껄이고 나서 돌아서 들어간다. 이 집의 인심은 후하구나. 다른 집 같으면 으레 한두 번은 가라고 할 터인데 하고, 으쓱해서 안을 보았다.

올려다 보이는 퇴 위에 높직이 앉은 방은 사랑인 듯했고, 그 옆으로 조그만 대문이 좀 삐딱해 보이고, 그리고 안 대청마루가 잠깐 보인다. 사랑채 왼편으로 죽 달려 이 문간에 와서 멈춘 방은 얼른 보아 창고인 듯, 앞으로 밀짚 낟가리들이 태산같이 가리어 있다. 밀짚대에서 빗방울이 다룽다룽 떨어진다. 약간 누런빛을 띠었다. 뜰이 휘휘하게 넓은데 빗물이 골이 져서 흘러내린다.

저리로 들어가야 밥술이나 얻어먹을 텐데, 그는 빗발 속에 보이는 안대문을 바라보고 서먹서먹한 발길을 옮겼다. 중대문을 들어서자, 안부엌으로부터 개 한 마리

such a good garment and looked directly into his smiling eyes. The man did not look like one who would try to snatch away other beggars' earnings. Ch'ilsŏng dropped his glance and looked at the water dripping from his sleeves. The man walked toward him, leaning on his crutch.

"Why are you standing there like that? Put this on."

"Oh, no." Ch'ilsŏng retreated one step and looked at the western jacket. His heart throbbed before a garment the like of which he had never worn in his life.

"Oh, aren't you a stubborn fellow! Then come here and sit on this mat." The man led him by the hand and made him sit on the straw mat. The man pretended not to notice Ch'ilsŏng's twisted legs.

"Have you eaten anything for breakfast?"

Ch'ilsŏng was fearful lest the man wanted a share in any food he might have in his sack, and cast a glance at the sack. It was dripping also.

"No."

After a silence, the man murmured, "Then you've got to eat something."

He searched his bundle for a while. "Here. Eat this, though it's only a trifle." He took out and

가 쏜살같이 달려나온다.

으르룽 하고 달려들므로 그는 개를 어를 양으로 주춤 물러서서 혀를 쩍쩍 채었다. 개는 날카로운 이를 내놓고 뛰어오르며 동냥자루를 확 물고 늘어진다. 그는 아찔하여 소리를 지르고 중문 밖으로 튀어나오자, 사랑에 사람이 있나 살피며 개를 꾸짖어 줬으면 했으나 잠잠하였다. 개는 눈을 뒤집고서 앞발을 버티고 뛰어오른다. 칠성이는 동냥자루를 잎에 물고 몸을 굽혔다 폈다 하다가도 못 이겨서 비슬비슬 쫓겨나왔다. 개는 여전히 따라 큰 대문에 와서는 칠성이가 용이히 움직이지 않으므로 으르렁 달려들어 잠방이 가랑이를 물고 늘어진다. 그는 악 소리를 자르고 달려나왔다. 아까 나왔던 사나이가 시멀시멀 웃으며 안으로부터 나왔다.

"워리워리."

개는 들은 체하지 않고 삐죽한 주둥이로 자꾸 짖었다. 저놈의 개를 죽일 수가 없을까 하는 마음이 부쩍 일어 그는 획 돌아서서 노려볼 때 사내는 손짓을 하여 개를 부른다. 그러니 개는 슬금슬금 물러나면서도 칠성에게서 눈을 떼지 않았다.

spread before Ch'ilsŏng something wrapped in a piece of newspaper. Inside the newspaper was some half dried-up boiled millet.

His appetite suddenly whetted by the sight of food, Ch'ilsŏng stretched out his hand to take it, but his hand did not work. It just shook. The man noticed it and placed the paper on Ch'ilsŏng's raised knees close to his mouth, saying, "I'm sorry there's so little."

Shyness weighed heavily on Ch'ilsŏng's eyelids, so he looked down, sniffed to hide his embarrassment, and sucked in the millet on the paper placed on his raised knees. The smell of printer's ink spread in his mouth and the slightly spoiled millet tasted sweeter the more he chewed it. As he smacked his lips over the last grain, his tongue yearned for more. His ears felt itchy and hot.

The man regretted there was no more. Ch'ilsŏng took his mouth away from the newspaper and smiled at him. The man smiled, too, and turning his eyes caught sight of Ch'ilsŏng's leg.

"Oh, you're bleeding! You must have hurt yourself!" He stooped down to look at it. Ch'ilsŏng felt the pain reviving and looked at it, too. His trouser leg was soaked red with blood and his leg had be-

갑자기 속이 메슥해지고 등허리가 오싹하더니 온몸에 열이 화끈 오른다. 개를 찾았으나 보이지 않고, 큰 대문만이 보기 싫게 버티고 있었다. 또 가볼까 하는 맘이 다소 머리를 드나, 그 개를 만날 것을 생각하니 진저리가 났다. 해서 단념하고 시죽시죽 걸었다.

비는 바람에 섞이어 모질게 갈겨 치고, 나무 흔들리는 소리, 도랑물 흐르는 소리에 귀가 뺑뺑할 지경이다. 붉은 물이 이리 몰리고 저리 몰리는 그 위엔 밀짚이 허옇게 떠 있고, 파랑새 같은 나뭇잎이 뱅글뱅글 떠돌아간다.

비에 젖은 옷은 사정없이 몸에 착 달라붙고 지동[4]치듯 부는 바람결에 숨이 흑흑 막혔다. 어쩔까 하고 둘러보았으나 집집이 문을 꼭 잠그고 아침 연기만 풀풀 피우고 있다. 혹 빈집이나 방앗간 같은 게 없나 했으나 눈에 뜨이지 않고, 무거운 눈엔 그 개가 자꾸만 얼른거리고 또 뒤에 다우쳐 오는 것 같다. 개에게 찢긴 잠방이 가랑이가 걸음에 따라 너덜너덜하여 그의 누런 다리 마디가 환히 들여다보이고, 푹 눌러쓴 밀짚모자에선 방울져 떨어지는 빗방울이 눈물같이 건건한 것을 입술에 느꼈다. 문득 그는 큰년의 옷감이 젖는구나 생각되자, 소리

gun to bleed once more. Suddenly he felt a pain in his bowels, and bent his leg and raised his head. He felt as if he were smelling the fishy smell of wet dogs in the wind.

"I got bitten by a dog."

"Oh, have you been to that tile-roofed house? The house that raises those bloody dogs? And there's more than one, too. Let me look at it. You mustn't leave a dog bite unattended."

The man grasped his leg. Ch'ilsŏng quickly pulled away but felt a smarting sensation across the bridge of his nose. He twitched his nose a couple of times. Tears ran down his cheeks. The man noticed that, and laughed and patted him on the back.

"Are you crying? If one were to cry at every... Well, you mustn't cry."

Ch'ilsŏng raised his head quickly to look at the man. The man's eyes were full of fury. When his eyes traveled to his leg again, Ch'ilsŏng felt heavy in the chest and dry in his throat. He dropped his head and, scooping up soft dust that lay piled on the floor, rubbed it on the wound.

"Oh, no! Don't ever do that again. Leave it alone if you don't have any ointment. Don't rub dirt on wounds again. That makes them fester."

를 내어 칵 울고 싶었다.

그는 우뚝 섰다. 들은 자욱하여 어디가 산인지 물인지 길인지 분간할 수 없고, 곡식대들이 미친 듯이 날뛰는 그 속으로 무슨 큰 짐승이 윙윙 우는 듯한 그런 크고도 둥근 소리가 대지를 울린다.

지금 그는 빗발에 따라 확확 일어나는 어떤 반항을 전신에 느끼면서 마음만은 앞으로 앞으로 가고 싶은데 발길이 딱 붙고 떨어지지 않는다. 돌아보니 동네도 거반 지나온 셈이요, 앞으로 조그만 집이 두셋이 남아 있다. 그리로 발길을 돌렸으나, 저 들에 미련이 남아 있는 듯 자주자주 멍하니 들을 바라보았다.

그가 개에게 쫓긴 것이 이번뿐이 아니오, 때로는 같은 사람한테도 학대와 모욕을 얼마든지 당하였건만, 오늘 일은 웬일인지 견딜 수 없는 분을 일으키게 된다.

"이 친구, 왜 그러구 섰수."

그는 놀라 보니 자기는 어느덧 조그만 집 앞에 섰고, 그 조그만 집은 연자간이라는 것을 알았다. 머리를 넘석하여 내다보는 사내는 얼른 보아 사오십 되었겠고 자기와 같은 불구자인 거지라는 것을 즉석에서 알았다.

Ch'ilsŏng bent his leg from embarrassment and looked out. The man was sunk in thought again.

Wind whipped in the rain, and the countless spiders' webs hanging from the ceiling swayed like smoke. The leaves of the willow tree shook like a frightened child and muddy water ran along the earth in a torrent. He looked up, startled to see a big bat covered with white chaff flapping its wings threateningly.

"Are you a born cripple?" the man asked suddenly. Ch'ilsŏng bowed his head and, after much hesitation, answered, "No."

"Then it was because of an illness. Did you get any treatment?"

Ch'ilsŏng looked long at his legs again, hesitating. At last he muttered, "No. None at all."

"Ugh, in this world sound legs get broken. It's nothing unusual not to get treatment for illness." The man laughed into the void. The laughter made Ch'ilsŏng shudder. He glanced at the man. As the man looked out at the road with fiercely dilated eyes, blue veins bulged on his forehead and his mouth was clenched shut. "Oh, I curse myself to think what a fool I was! I should have fought till death! What a damned stupid fool I was!"

사내는 쫑긋이 웃는다. 그는 이리 찾아오고도 저 사나이를 보니 들어가고 싶지 않아 머뭇거리다가도 하는 수 없이 들어갔다. 쌀겨내 가득히 흐르는 그 속에 말똥내도 훅훅 풍겼다.

"이리 오우, 저 옷이 젖어서 원……."

사내는 나무다리를 짚고 일어나서 깔고 앉았던 거적자리를 다시 펴고 자리를 내놓고 비켜 앉는다. 칠성이는 얼른 히뜩히뜩 센 머리털과 수염을 보고 늙은 것이 내 동냥해 온 것을 빼앗으려나 하는 겁이 나고 싫어졌다.

"그 옷 땜에 춥겠수. 우선 내 헌 옷을 입고 벗어서 말리우."

사나이는 그의 보따리를 뒤적뒤적 하더니,

"자 입소. 이리 오우."

칠성이는 돌아보았다. 시커먼 양복인데 군데군데 기운 것이다. 그 순간 어디서 좋은 옷 얻었는데, 나두 저런 게나 얻었으면, 하면서 이상한 감정에 싸여 사나이의 웃는 눈을 정면으로 보았을 때 동냥자루나 뺏을 사람 같지 않았다. 그는 머리를 숙이고 소매에서 떨어지는 물방울을 보았다. 사나이는 나무다리를 짚고 이리로 온다.

Ch'ilsŏng pricked up his ears and tried to understand the meaning of the man's words, but could not make it out. The man looked back at Ch'ilsŏng. The two or three thin wrinkles under his eyes reminded Ch'ilsŏng of his own father.

"Listen, my boy. I was the head of a family once. I was a model worker in a factory, too. A first-rate engineer. After my leg was broken I was thrown out of the factory, and my woman ran away and the children cried from hunger. My parents died of sorrow. Oh, there's no use talking about it."

The man stared at Ch'ilsŏng. Ch'ilsŏng's heart pounded for some reason and he could not meet the man's eyes, so he looked at his broken leg, and at the mute earth under that leg.

Outside it was misty with drizzling rain, and the distant mountain looked tearful. The croaking of frogs gave him the illusion of being in his own village, and he fancied himself looking at Kŭnnyŏn's back under the locust tree. Ch'ilsŏng got up.

"I've got to go home."

The man got up, too.

"Oh, do you have a home? Then go."

When Ch'ilsŏng raised his head the man came near him and arranged his straw hat for him, smil-

"왜 그러구 섰수. 자 입으시우."

"아아니유."

칠성이는 성큼 물러서서 양복저고리를 보았다. 나서 생전 입어보지 못한 그 옷 앞에 어쩐지 가슴까지 두근거린다.

"허! 그 친구 고집 대단한데, 그럼, 이리 와 앉기나 해유."

사나이는 그의 손을 끌고 거적자리로 와서 앉힌다. 눈결에 사내의 뭉퉁한 다리를 보고 못 본 것처럼 하였다.

"아침 자셨수."

칠성이는 이 자가 내 동냥자루에 아침 얻어온 줄로 알고 이러는가 하여, 힐끔 동냥자루를 보았다. 거기에서도 물이 떨어지고 있다.

"아니유."

사내는 잠잠하였다가,

"안되었구려. 뭘 좀 먹어야 할 터인데……."

사내는 또 무슨 생각을 하는 듯하더니, 그의 보따리를 뒤진다.

"자, 이것 적지만 자시유."

ing. Ch'ilsŏng felt like leaning on him as if he were his mother.

"Goodbye. Hope to see you again."

Instead of answering, Ch'ilsŏng smiled at him and left. When he looked back after a long time the man was standing there before the mill, absently. Ch'ilsŏng wiped away his tears with his fist and looked back again.

The patches of millet and Indian millet fields were flooded with rain, and the stalks were half sunk under water. A frog croaked, and he thought to himself this was going to be a lean year again. The croaking of the frog sounded like the heavy groan of a man.

It began to drizzle again. His clothes that got wet once more and the rain weighing down his eyelashes made his heart heavy with swirling indefinable misgivings.

When he reached his village the rain thickened again and the wind also began to blow. Even the locust tree that always looked cool seemed gloomy under the scowling sky, and the low mountains screening the back of the village looked dim through the rain. His steps faltered when the hedges of the houses and the vegetable gardens

신문지에 싼 것을 내들어 펴보인다. 그 종이엔 노란 조밥이 고실고실 말라가고 있다.

밥을 보니 구미가 버쩍 당기어 부지중에 손을 내밀었으나, 손이 말을 안 듣고 떨리어서 흠칫하였다. 사나이는 이 눈치를 채었음인지, 종이를 그의 입 가까이 갖다 대고,

"적어 안되었수."

부끄럼이 눈썹 끝에 일어 칠성이는 눈을 내려 뜨고 애꿎이 코를 들여마시며 종이를 무릎에 놓고 입을 대고 핥아먹었다. 신문지내가 이 사이에 나들고 약간 쉰 듯한 밥알이 씹을수록 고소하였다. 입맛을 다실 때마다 좀더 있으면 하는 아쉬운 마음이 혀끝에 날름거리고 사내 편을 향한 귓바퀴가 어쩐지 가려운 듯 따가움을 느꼈다.

"적어서 원……."

사내의 이러한 말을 들으며 신문지에서 입을 떼고 히하고 웃어 보이었다. 사내도 따라 웃고 무심히 칠성의 다리를 보았다.

"어디 다쳤나 보! 피가 나우."

came into view, and when he thought that Kŭnnyŏn might be going to the well below the mountain with the water jar on her head.

When he arrived home his mother came out to meet him with eyes full of tears.

"Oh, you bad boy! Where have you been all this while? Didn't you ever think your mother'd be waiting?" Taking the sack from him, his mother wept. Ch'ilsŏng didn't answer, but came into the room where the floor was more than half covered with bowls and basins for catching the rain leaking from the ceiling. The water hit the bowls and basins rhythmically. Ch'ilsŏng stood there and didn't know what to do. He shivered and shook more severely from cold than when he had been walking.

Ch'il-un and the baby were lying on the floor, and the baby's head was wrapped round with some whitish cloth. On their small bodies too the water fell.

"Sit down somewhere. Oh, I roamed the town all night last night searching for you. I even looked into taverns and bars. You bad boy, why didn't you tell me you'd be away if you weren't coming back at night?"

허리를 굽히어 들여다본다. 칠성은 얼른 아픔을 느끼고 들여다보니 잠방이 가랑에 피가 빨갛게 묻었고 다리엔 방금 선혈이 흐르고 있다. 별안간 속이 무쭉해서[5] 그는 다리를 움츠리고 머리를 들었다. 바람결에 개비린내 같은 것이 훌씬 끼친다.

"개, 개한테 그리 되었지우."

"아, 그 기와집에 가셨수…… 그놈네 개를 길러도 흉악한 개를 기르거든 흥! 돈 있는 놈이라 모두 한 놈이 아니우. 어디 이리 내놓우. 개에게 물린 것이 심상히 여길 것이 못 되우."

사내는 그의 다리를 잡아당기었다. 그는 얼른 다리를 치우면서도 형용할 수 없는 울분이 젖은 옷에까지 오싹오싹 기어오르고 코 안이 싸해서 몇 번 코를 움직일 때, 뜻하지 않은 눈물이 주르르 흘러내린다. 사내는 이 눈치를 채고 허허 웃으면서 그의 등을 가볍게 두드렸다.

"이 친구 우오. 울기로 하자면…… 허허 울어선 못 쓰오. 난 공장에서 생생하던 이 자리가 기계에 물려 이리 되었소만, 지금 세상이 어떤 줄 아시우."

칠성이는 머리를 번쩍 들어 사내를 바라보니 눈에 분

His mother wept aloud now. Since she had lost her husband she leaned on her crippled son as the pillar of the family. Ch'il-un woke up from the noise.

"Oh, it's Brother! Brother's back!" He jumped up, rubbing his eyes. Swarms of flies flew up, and the baby fretted. Ch'il-un rubbed his eyes with both hands and tried to look at his brother but couldn't, so he rubbed harder.

"Oh, son, don't. That will hurt you more. Oh, the children have been sick while you were away and made me so worried. And Ch'il-un's got those sore eyes, too. I wonder what's come over this village. Everybody, young and old, has sore eyes."

None of these words came to Ch'ilsŏng's ears. He dearly wished to lie down somewhere where water did not fall and go to sleep. Ch'il-un broke out crying from irritation and then, going out the back door, urinated and washed his eyes with the urine.

"Wet your eyes well. Not just the lids but the eyeballs, too. Look how he wants to look at you. He asked for his brother all day yesterday." His mother wept again. Ch'ilsŏng moved aside to avoid the water dripping on his back. This time water dropped on his nose and ran down to his lips. He

노의 빛이 은은하였다. 다시 다리로 시선이 옮겨질 때, 가슴이 턱 막히고 목에 무엇이 가로 질리는 것 같아 시름없이 머리를 숙이고 무심히 부드러운 먼지를 쥐어 상처에 발랐다.

"어이구! 먼지를 바르면 되우?"

사내는 칠성의 손을 꽉 붙들었다. 칠성이는 어린애같이 웃고 나서,

"이러면 나아유."

"아 원, 그런 일 다시는 하지 마우. 약이 없으면 말지, 그런 일 하면 되우. 더 성해서 앓게 되우."

칠성이는 약간 무안해서 다리를 움츠리고 밖을 바라보았다. 사내는 또다시 무슨 생각에 깊이 잠기는 것 같다.

바람이 비를 안고 싸싸 밀려들고, 천장의 수없는 거미줄은 끊어져 연기같이 나부꼈다. 바라 뵈는 버드나무의 잎은 팔팔 떨고 아래로 시뻘건 물이 콸콸 소리를 내고 흐른다. 어깨 위가 어찔해서 돌아보면 큰 맷돌이 쌀겨를 뽀얗게 쓰고서 얼음 같은 서늘한 기를 품품 피우고 있다.

"배 안의 병신이우?"

struck his nose angrily and swore.

"Oh, why should it rain now? And the wind! What fierce wind! It will break all the millet stalks. Oh, God, what can be done?" She raised her clasped hands as if in prayer. Her hair was all matted with the rain, and her eyes were bloodshot, the eyelids blue-black and sunken. Her soiled clothes were stained with rain.

Ch'ilsŏng sat down on the sill and closed his eyes. His eyes felt unbearably sore and his eyelashes stung his eyeballs. As he rolled his eyes a couple of times, he suddenly recalled the water-mill.

"Yesterday the dike of Kaettong's rice paddy broke and everything was swept away. Oh, what a dreadful curse is that wind! What's going to happen to our field?"

His mother ran outside. Ch'il-un, crying, tried to follow her but tripped on the doorsill, fell down on the ground and screamed. Ch'ilsŏng raised his eyebrows. "I'll kill that thing.'"

His mother quickly picked Ch'il-un up to take him out of her older son's sight and walked around in and out, casting anxious eyes toward their field.

Ch'ilsŏng did not want to see his worried mother, so he turned aside and closed his eyes. Startled, he

사내는 문득 이렇게 물었다. 칠성이는 머리를 숙이고 머뭇머뭇하다가,

"아 아니유."

"그럼 앓다가 그리 되었구려…… 약 써 봤수?"

칠성이는 또다시 말하기가 힘든 듯이 우물쭈물하고 다리만 보았다. 한참 후에,

"아아니유, 못못 썼어유."

"흥! 말짱한 생다리도 꺾이우는 지경인데 약 못 쓰는 것쯤이야, 허허."

사내는 허공을 향하여 웃는다. 그 웃음소리에 소름이 오싹 끼쳐 힐끔 사내를 보았다. 눈을 무섭게 뜨고 밖을 내다보는데, 이마엔 퍼런 힘줄이 불쑥 일었고, 입은 꼭 다물고 있다.

"허, 치가 떨려서. 내 왜 그리 어리석었던지. 지금만 같으면 지금이라면 죽더라도 해볼걸. 왜 그 꼴이었어! 흥!"

칠성이는 귀를 밝혀 이 말을 새겨들으려 했으나 무엇을 의미한 말인지 알 수가 없었다. 사내는 칠성이를 돌아보았다. 눈 아래 두어 줄의 주름살이 돌아가신 그의

opened his eyes. The baby, who had been lying in a corner of the room drawing quick breaths, tried to get up and fell down repeatedly, weeping. She kept rubbing her head on the straw mat and fretfully scratched the cloth wound round her head, making a sound that made him feel creepy.

Ch'ilsŏng tried not to open his eyes but he could not help opening them and catching sight of the baby's yellow fingers tearing at her head. He wished the baby dead, and closed his eyes.

Wind blew more fiercely. One could hear the branches of the apricot tree breaking, and also a sound like a pillar toppling that shook the back door. Ch'il-un came into the room and lay down.

"Brother, get me some eye medicine tomorrow. Kaettong's father bought him eye medicine from the town and his eyes are all right now."

Ch'ilsŏng listened to his brother in silence and thought of the fabric inside his shirt. The thought that he should have bought eye medicine instead crossed his mind but quickly disappeared, and he tried to think of a way to give the cloth to Kŭnnyŏn.

A match struck in the kitchen and soon his mother came in.

"Water got into the stove, up to the top. What can

아버지와 흡사했다.

"이 친구, 나두 한 가정을 가졌던 놈이우. 공장에선 모범공인이었구. 허허 모범공인!…… 다리가 꺾인 후에 돈 한푼 못 가지고 공장에서 나오니 계집은 달아나고 어린것들은 배고파 울고 부모는 근심에 근심에 지레 돌아가시구…… 허 말해서 뭘 하우. 우리를 이렇게 못살게 하는 놈이 저 하늘인 줄 아우? 이 땅인 줄 아우?"

사내는 칠성이를 딱 쏘아본다. 어쩐지 칠성의 가슴은 까닭 없이 두근거려 차마 사내를 정면으로 보지 못하고 꺾인 다리를 보았다. 그리고 사내의 다리 밑에 황소같이 말없는 땅을 보았다.

"아니우, 결코 아니우. 비록 우리가 이 꼴이 되어 전전걸식은 하지만두. 왜 우리가 이 꼴이 되었는지나 알아야 하지 않소……. 내 다리를 꺾에 한 놈두, 친구를 저런 병신으로 되게 한 놈두, 다 누구겠소? 알아들었수? 이 친구."

사나이의 이 같은 말은 칠성의 뼈끝마다 짤짤 저리게 하였고, 애꿎은 하늘과 땅만 저주하던 캄캄한 속에 어떤 번쩍하는 불빛을 던져주는 것 같으면서도 다시 생각

I do? The little ones haven't had anything yet, either. How hungry you all must be!" She went out and came running back presently.

"The dike broke in Kŭnnyŏn's rice paddy, too. The strongest dike in the neighborhood. Oh, what's going to happen to ours?"

Ch'ilsŏng's eyes became dilated.

"Oh, why doesn't this little girl go to sleep? Don't tear at your head like that! That little girl hasn't slept a wink for days. Kaettong's mother told me rat skin's good for sores so I killed one and plastered its skin on her head, but she keeps tearing at it like that. I guess it itches because it's healing. Don't you think so?" His mother seemed to want some reassuring concurrence. But Ch'ilsŏng didn't want to hear about anything except Kŭnnyŏn. He asked patiently, "Then everything's swept away in their rice fields?"

"Yes! Oh my milk's dried up." Looking at the fretting baby, his mother massaged her breasts. They were limp.

The baby panted more urgently and her hands tried to reach her head but dropped down tiredly. His mother listened again to the sound of the wind.

"Oh, our millet will all be swept away now! Our

하면 아찔해지고 팽팽 돌아간다. 무엇인가 묻고 싶어 머리를 번쩍 들었으나 입이 꽉 붙고 만다. 그는 시름없이 하늘을 물끄러미 보았다.

어느덧 밖은 안개비로 자욱하였고 먼 산이 눈물을 머금고 구불구불 솟아 있으며, 빗소리에 잠겼던 개구리 소리가 그의 동네 앞인가도 싶게 했고, 또한 큰년의 뒷매가 홰나무 아래 얼른거려 보인다. 칠성이는 부시시 일어났다.

"난 난 집에 가겠수."

사내는 따라 일어난다.

"아, 집이 있수? ……가보우."

칠성이는 머리를 드니, 사내가 곁에 와서 밀짚모자를 잘 씌워주고 빙긋이 웃는다. 어머니를 대한 것처럼 어딘가 모르게 의지하고 싶은 생각과 믿는 맘이 들었다.

"잘 가우…… 세월 좋으면 또 만나지……."

대답 대신으로 그는 마주 웃어 보이고 걸었다. 한참이나 오다가 돌아보니 사내는 우두커니 서 있다. 주먹으로 눈을 닦고 보고 또 보았다.

길 좌우에 늘어앉은 조밭 수수밭은 이랑마다 물이 충

field can't escape a flood if Kŭnnyŏn's field got swept away. Oh, Kŭnnyŏn's lucky she doesn't have to live through this. She got married yesterday."

"What?" Ch'ilsŏng screamed. The precious fabric kept inside his shirt struck his skin like a rock. His mother looked at her son, startled.

"Mum, look at that!" Ch'il-un jumped up and groaned. They all looked.

The cloth wrapped around the baby's head was about half torn off, and maggots as big as rice grains were crawling out of it.

"Oh, God! What happened? What happened?" His mother went over to the baby and snatched away the cloth. The rat skin came away and from it dropped masses of maggots bathed in blood.

"Baby! My baby! Wake up! Oh, wake up!" Hearing his mother's scream, Ch'ilsŏng ran outside frenziedly.

Rain poured down fiercely and wind stormed madly, and the sky, torn mercilessly by the lightning, roared with thunder.

Ch'ilsŏng glared up at the sky.

* From *The Rainy Spell and Other Korean Stories* (rev. and exp. ed.), ed. and trans. Suh Ji-moon (Armonk, NY: M.E. Sharpe, 1998), 77-106. Translation copyright © 1998 by Suh Ji-moon. Used

충했고, 조이삭 수수이삭이 절반 넘어져 물에 잠겨 있다. 올해도 흉년이구나 할 때 어디서 "맹" 하니 또 어디서 "꽁" 하는 소리가 들렸다. 저 멀리 귀 시끄럽게 우짖는 개구리 소리는 무심한데, 이제 그 어딘가 곁에서 "맹꽁"한 그 소리는 사람의 음성같이 무게가 있었다.

안개비 나실나실 내려온다. 조금 말라오려던 옷이 또 촉촉히 젖고 눈썹 끝에 안개비 엉키어 마음까지 묵중하고 알 수 없는 의문이 뒤범벅이 되어 돌아간다.

그가 그의 마을까지 왔을 때는 다시 빗발이 굵어지고 바람이 슬슬 불기 시작하였다. 언제나 시원해 보이는 홰나무도 찡그린 하늘 아래 우울해 있고, 동네 뒤로 나지막이 둘러 있는 산도 빗발에 묻히어 잘 보이지 않았다. 그러나 큰년이가 물동이를 이고 이 비를 맞으면서도 저 산 아래 박우물로 달려가지나 않나 하는 생각이, 집집의 울바자며 채마밭의 긴바자가 차츰 선명히 보일 때 선뜻 들어 그의 발길은 허둥거렸다.

집에까지 오니 어머니는 눈물이 그득해서 나왔다.

"이놈아, 어미 기다릴 것도 생각지 않고 어딜 그리 다니느냐."

Translated by Suh Ji-moon

어머니는 동냥자루를 받아 쥐고 쿨쩍쿨쩍 울었다. 칠성이는 잠잠히 방으로 들어오니, 빗물 받는 그릇으로 절반 차지했고 뚝뚝 듣는 빗소리가 장단 맞춰 났다. 칠성이는 그만 우두커니 서서 어쩔 줄을 몰랐다. 몸은 아까보다 더 춥고 떨리어서 견딜 수 없다.

칠운이와 아기는 아랫목에 누워 있고 아기 머리엔 무슨 헝겊으로 허옇게 싸매 있었다. 그들의 그 작은 몸에도 빗방울이 간혹 떨어진다.

“아무 데나 앉으렴. 어쩌겠니…… 에그, 난 어젯밤 널 찾아 읍에 가서 밤새 싸다니다 왔다. 오죽해야 술집 문까지 두드렸겠니? 이놈아 어딜 가면 간다고 하지 그게 뭐야.”

이번에는 소리까지 내어 운다.

남편을 잃은 뒤 그나마 저 병신 아들을 하늘같이 중히 의지해 살아가는 어머니의 맘을 엿볼 수가 있다. 칠운이는 울음소리에 벌떡 일어났다.

“성 왔네! 성 왔네!”

눈을 잔뜩 움켜쥐고 뛰었다. 그 통에 파리는 우구구 끓고 아기까지 키성키성 보채인다. 칠운이는 두 손으로 눈을 비비치고 형을 보려다는 못 보고 또 비비친다.

"이 새끼야, 고만두라구. 그러니 더 아프지. 에그 너 없는 새 저것들이 자꾸만 앓아서 죽겠다. 거게다 눈까지 덧치니, 그런데 이 동리는 웬일이냐. 지금 눈병 때문에 큰일이구나. 아이 어른이 모두 눈병에 걸려 눈을 못 뜬다."

칠성이는 지금 아무 말도 귀에 거치지 않고 비 새지 않는 곳에 누워 한잠 푹 들고 싶었다. 칠운이는 마침내 응응 울다가 무슨 생각을 하고 뒷문 밖으로 나가더니 오줌을 내 뻗치우며 그 오줌을 눈에 바른다.

"잘 발라라. 눈등에만 바르지 말고 눈 속에까지 발러……. 저것도 보고 반가와서 저리도 눈을 뜨려누나. 어제는 성아 성아 찾더구나."

어머니는 또 운다. 칠성이는 등에 선뜻 떨어지는 빗방울에 피하여 앉으니 이번엔 콧등에 떨어져 입술로 흐른다. 그는 콧등을 후려치고 화를 버럭 내었다.

"제 제길!"

"글쎄 비는 왜 오겠니. 바람이나 불지 말아야 할 터인데 저 바람! 기껏 키운 조는 다 쓰러져 싹이 나겠구나.

아이구 이 노릇을 어찌해야 좋으냐. 하느님 맙시사!"

두 손을 곧추 들고 애걸한다. 그의 머리는 비에 젖어 이마에 붙었고 눈은 눈꼽에 탁 엉키었고 그 속으로 핏줄이 빨겋게 일어 눈이 시큼해서 바라볼 수 없는데 시커먼 옷에 천정물이 어룽어룽 젖었다.

칠성이는 얼른 샛문 턱에 걸터앉아 눈을 딱 감아버렸다. 눈이 자꾸만 피곤하고 그래선지 속눈썹이 가시같이 눈 속을 꼭꼭 찌른다.

그는 눈을 두어 번 굴렸을 때 문득 방앗간이 떠오른다.

"어제 개똥네 논에 동이 터졌는데 전부 쓸려 나갔다누나. 에구 무서워. 저게 무슨 바람이냐. 저 바람! 우리 밭은 어쩌나."

어머니는 밖으로 뛰어나간다. 칠운이는 울면서 따르다가 문턱에 걸려 공중 나가 넘어지고 시재 까무러치는 소리를 하였다. 칠성이는 눈을 부릅떴다.

"저 저놈의 새끼, 주 죽이고 말까부다."

어머니는 얼른 칠운이를 업고 물러나서 정신없이 밖을 바라보고, 또 나갔다가 들어왔다. 칠운이를 때리다가 중얼중얼하며 돌아간다.

칠성이는 이 꼴이 보기 싫어 모로 앉아 눈을 감았다. 무엇에 놀라 눈을 뜨니, 아랫목에 누워 할딱할딱하는 아기가 일어나려다 쓰러지고 소리 없는 울음을 입으로 운다. 머리를 갈자리에 비비치다가도 시원치 않은지 손이 올라가서 헝겊을 쥐고 박박 할퀴는 소리란 징그러워 들을 수 없었다.

칠성이는 눈을 안 뜨자 하다가도 어느새 문득 뜨게 되고 아기의 저 노란 손가락이 머리를 쥐어뜯는 것을 보게 된다. 조놈의 계집애는 죽었으면! 하면서 눈을 감는다.

바람은 점점 더 세차게 분다. 살구나무 꺾이는 소리가 뚝뚝 나고 집 기둥이 쏠리는지 씩컥 쿵! 하는 소리가 샛문에 울렸다. 칠운이는 방으로 들어와서 눕는다.

"성아, 내일은 눈약두 얻어오렴. 개똥이는 저 아버지가 읍에 가서 눈약 사왔다는데, 저 그 약을 넣으니까, 눈이 나았다더라 응야."

칠성이는 잠잠히 들으며, 얼른 가슴에 품겨 있는 큰년의 옷감을 생각하였다. 차라리 눈약이나 사올 것을 하는 마음이 잠깐 들었으나 사라지고 어떻게 큰년에게 이 옷감을 들려줄까 하였다.

부엌에서 성냥 긋는 소리가 들리더니, 어머니가 들어온다.

"아궁에 물이 가득하니 이를 어쩌냐. 저것들도 아무것도 못 먹었는데…… 너두 배고프겠구나."

이런 말을 하고 밖으로 나가더니 곧 뛰어들어온다.

"큰년네 논두 동이 터졌단다. 그리 튼튼하던 동두, 저를 어쩌니."

칠성이는 눈을 둥그렇게 떴다.

"좀 자려무나, 요 계집애야 왜 자꾸만 머리를 뜯니, 조놈의 계집애는 며칠째 안 자고 새웠단다. 개똥 어머니가 쥐가죽이 약이라기 쥐를 잡아 저리 붙였는데 자꾸만 떼려구 저러니, 아마 나을려구 가려운 모양이지."

그렇다고 해줘야 어머니는 맘이 놓일 모양이다. 큰년네 말에 칠성이는 눈을 떴는데 딴 푸념을 하니 듣기 싫었다. 하나 꾹 참고,

"그 그래. 큰년네두 논이 떴대?"

"그래! 젖이 안 나니……."

어머니는 연신 아기를 보고 그의 젖을 주물러본다. 명

주 고름끈같이 말큰거린다.

아기는 점점 더 할딱할딱 숨이 차오고 이젠 손을 놀릴 기운도 없는지 손이 귀밑으로 올라가고는 맥을 잃고 다르르 굴러 떨어진다. 어머니는 바람 소리를 듣더니,

"이전 우리 조는 못 쓰게 되었겠다! 큰년네 논이 뜨는데 견디겠니……. 참 큰년이는 복 좋아, 글쎄 이런 꼴 안 보렴인지 어제 시집갔단다."

"큰년이가?"

칠성이는 버럭 소리쳤다. 그의 가슴에 고이 안겨 있던 큰년의 옷감은 돌같이 딱 맞질리운다. 어머니는 아들의 태도에 놀라 바라보았다.

"어마이! 저것 봐!"

칠운이는 뛰어 일어나서 응응 운다. 그들은 놀라 일시에 바라보았다.

아기는 언제 그 헝겊을 찢었는지 반쯤 헝겊이 찢어졌고 그리로부터 쌀알 같은 구더기가 설렁설렁 내달아오고 있다.

"아이구머니. 이게 웬일이야 응, 이게 웬일이어!"

어머니는 와락 기어가서 헝겊을 잡아 제치니 쥐가죽

이 딸려 일어나고 피를 문 구더기가 아글바글 떨어진다.

"아가 아가 눈 떠, 눈 떠라, 아가!"

이 같은 어머니의 비명을 들으며 칠성이는 "엑!" 소리를 지르고 우둥퉁퉁 밖으로 나와 버렸다.

비는 좍좍 쏟아지고 바람은 미친 듯 몰아치는데 가다가 우르릉 쾅쾅 하고 하늘이 울고 번갯불이 제멋대로 쭉쭉 찢겨나가고 있다.

칠성이는 묵묵히 저 하늘을 노려보고 있었다.

1) '몽땅'을 구어적으로 이르는 말(북한어).
2) 바퀴벌레.
3) 반나절.
4) 지진.
5) '묵직하다'의 방언.

* 작가 고유의 문체나 당시 쓰이던 용어를 그대로 살려 원문에 최대한 가깝게 표기하고자 하였다. 단, 현재 쓰이지 않는 말이나 띄어쓰기는 현행 맞춤법에 맞게 표기하였다.

《조선일보》, 1936

해설

Afterword

가난의 생태학, 비체화된 몸

김양선 (문학평론가)

'식민지 시대 빈궁문학의 대표작', '하층민의 삶을 그린 리얼리즘의 수작'이라고 평가받는 강경애의 「지하촌」. 소설 제목이 암시하듯이 이 소설은 '지하'와 같은 어두운 식민지 현실을 여성과 아이, 장애인을 비롯한 사회적 약자의 처지에 초점을 맞추어 그리고 있다.

강경애의 소설 대부분이 작가가 결혼 후 정착했던 간도를 배경으로 이주민의 현실을 다루었던 데 반해 「지하촌」은 작가의 고향인 송화로 추정되는 가난한 농촌 마을이 배경이다. 어린 시절 아버지의 죽음으로 인한 가장의 부재, 학비조차 내지 못할 정도의 가난은 강경애 소설의 주 모티프이기도 하다. 「지하촌」에서도 가난

Ecology of Poverty and Abject Bodies

Kim Yang-sun (literary critic)

Often praised as "representative of 'poverty literature' during the colonial period" or "a masterfully realistic depiction of the underprivileged," Kang Kyŏng-ae's "The Underground Village" depicts the gloomy reality of colonial Chosun, focusing on weak members of society such as women, children, and the disabled.

Although most of Kang's works deal with the lives of migrant Koreans living in Jiandao, where Kang settled after her marriage, "The Underground Village" is set in a poverty-stricken farming village strongly reminiscent of her home village Song-hwa in Korea. Kang's own experience of losing her fa-

때문에 최소한의 염치나 도덕마저 잃어버린 채, 살아남기 그 자체가 목적이 되어 버린 식민지 농촌 현실을 충격적으로 형상화하고 있다.

이 소설은 '빈곤의 여성화(feminization of poverty)'라는 제3세계 여성의 상황을 전형적으로 보여준다. 가장이 없는 상태에서 가족의 생계를 책임지는 존재가 이 여성들이다. 주인공 칠성의 어머니, 큰년이의 어머니는 하루 종일 농사일에다 집에 와서도 아이를 돌보느라 쉴 틈이 없다. 큰년이의 어머니는 밭에서 일을 하다가 갑자기 아이를 낳게 되는데, 그 아이마저 죽어버린다. 칠성의 어머니는 아이를 낳자마자 그 다음 날부터 밭일을 나가느라 몸을 제대로 돌보지 못한 탓에 밑이 빠져서 "살덩이가 늘어져서 들어갈 줄 모르고 무슨 물을 줄줄 흘리고", 고약스런 악취와 염증에 시달린다. 큰년이는 돈푼이나 있다는 집에 첩으로 팔려간다. 가사노동과 농사일이라는 이중의 노동에 시달리는 여성, 가난과 고된 노동으로 인해 사산을 하거나 불구자들을 낳을 수밖에 없는 여성들이 생계를 전담해야 하는 현실, 눈 먼 딸이 팔려가는 것을 보면서도 이를 부러워하는, 도덕보다 생존이 앞서는 것이 바로 이 '지하촌'의 현실이다.

ther to illness, and the subsequent poverty that rendered her unable to afford school during her early childhood, are apparent in most of Kang's novels and short stories. "The Underground Village" also depicts the shockingly destitute living conditions of farming villages during the colonial period, wherein the villagers couldn't entertain the slightest sense of shame or decency in the face of a constant struggle for survival.

"The Underground Village" paints a typical picture of the "feminization of poverty" in the Third World, wherein a woman takes charge of her family's livelihood in the absence of a husband. Ch'ilsŏng's and Kŭnnyŏn's mothers do not have any time for rest because they have to work the farm all day, then take care of their children after work. Kŭnnyŏn's mother gives birth to a baby while working in the field, but the baby soon dies. Ch'ilsŏng's mother suffers from a nasty stench and inflammation, because she has to go to work immediately after giving birth. At a young age, Kŭnnyŏn is sold to a wealthy family as a concubine. In this underground village, women suffer because of their dual responsibilities in the home and on the farm. They give birth to dead or disabled babies because of

또한 이 소설은 사회적 약자인 아이들, 더구나 질병이 나 신체적 장애를 가진 아이들이 위생 상태나 최소한의 안전장치마저 없는 환경에서 살아가는 모습을 사실적으로 그리고 있다. 주인공인 칠성이는 손발이 뒤틀려서 제대로 쓸 수 없는 데다가 언어장애까지 있다. 그런데도 불편한 몸으로 이 동네, 저 동네를 다니면서 구걸을 해서 식구들을 먹여 살려야 하는 처지이다. 그가 짝사랑하는 큰년이는 어렸을 때 제때 치료를 받지 못해 시력을 잃었다. 칠성이의 어린 동생들도 영양실조로 시름시름 앓거나 몸 곳곳에 상처가 나 있다. 극도의 가난은 아이들의 심성마저 피폐하게 만들었다. 칠성이는 먹을 것만 밝히는 동생 칠운이나 아기를 미워하고, 심지어 때리고 욕설을 퍼붓는다. 동생 칠운이는 형이 불편한 몸으로 겨우겨우 구걸해서 가져온 먹을 것을 몰래 훔쳐 먹거나 아기를 제대로 돌보지 않는다. 그 어떤 것보다도 당장의 허기를 면하는 것이 이 아이들에게는 중요한 것이다.

작가는 이와 같은 식민지 농촌 현실의 문제점을 충격적으로 전달하기 위한 문학적 기법으로 그로테스크한 묘사를 사용하였다. "아기는 손을 깔고 봉당에 엎디어

their hard labor. They envy the family whose young blind daughter is sold as a concubine to a wealthy family. In this village, survival trumps everything, including minimal human decency.

This short story also realistically depicts another socially marginalized group: children—especially those children suffering from illness or disability, and living in an environment without hygiene or safety devices. Ch'ilsŏng, the protagonist of this story, suffers from a speech impediment and distorted limbs; however, he wanders around various villages, begging to support his family. He has a crush on Kŭnnyŏn, who loses her sight because she can't get proper treatment for an illness. Ch'ilsŏng's younger siblings suffer from malnutrition and various sores on their bodies. Extreme poverty distorts their characters, too. Ch'ilsŏng hates his younger siblings, Ch'il-un and "the baby," just because they want to eat. He even beats and curses at them. Not only does Ch'il-un steal the food his disabled brother procures by begging, but he also runs away from his baby sister now and then, though there is no one else to take care of her. For these children, quenching their immediate hunger is much more important than anything.

잠들었고, 게워 놓은 자리엔 쉬파리가 날개 없는 듯이 벌벌 기고 있으며, 아기 머리와 빠끔히 벌린 입에는 잔파리 왕파리가 아글바글 들싼다." "허벅다리엔 피가 흥건했고 또 주먹 같은 살덩이가 축 늘어져 있었다.(……) 그 살덩이가 오늘까지 늘어져서 들어갈 줄 모르고 또 무슨 물을 줄줄 흘리고 있다." "아기는 (상처난 머리에 붙인—필자 주) 언제 그 헝겊을 찢었는지 반쯤 헝겊이 찢어졌고 그리로부터 쌀알같은 구더기가 설렁설렁 내달아오고 있다"와 같은 구절에서 알 수 있듯이 최소한의 위생이나 의료적 처치마저도 갖춰지지 않은 짐승과 같은 상태에 이 가족들은 그야말로 내버려져 있는 것이다. 무지와 가난이 야기한 이 비참한 상황은 식민지 현실의 모순을 극적으로 드러내는 효과가 있다. 가난과 고된 노동으로 인해 사산을 하거나 불구자를 낳을 수밖에 없는 여성들의 몸 역시 피와 고름이 흐르는 비체화된 몸으로 형상화된다.

이들에게는 희망이 없다. 오히려 상황은 악화일로를 걷는다. 동냥을 나갔던 첫째 칠성이는 개에 물리고, 잠깐 비를 피하기 위해 들어간 연자간에서 우연히 공장 노동자로 일하다 다리를 다쳐 거지로 떠도는 사람을 만

The author uses grotesque images such as the following to depict this kind of village life under colonialism, intentionally shocking readers.

"the baby asleep on the dirt floor, head pillowed on hand. On her vomit flies were crawling, and on the baby's head and inside the baby's open mouth were swarms of flies." [...] "a lump of flesh as big as her fist was hanging down from her inside and blood was all over her thighs." [...] "The cloth wrapped around the baby's head was about half torn off, and maggots as big as rice grains were crawling out of it."

Here we clearly see the kind of degradingly atrocious situation the villagers were thrown into without any sort of basic hygienic or medical facilities, and the shameful reality of colonial Chosun. We also get a glimpse of the viewpoint that women who give birth to dead or disabled babies because of their poverty and ignorance are useless.

There is no hope for these villagers. Their situation moves from bad to worse. Ch'ilsŏng gets bitten by a dog while begging. Although Ch'ilsŏng shares a moment of sympathy with another beggar

나지만 상황에 대한 분노는 일시적인 감정에 그친다. 소설은 큰년이가 칠성의 바람과는 달리 이미 시집을 가서 마을을 떠난 데다가 칠성이의 동생들을 비롯하여 동네 전체가 눈병에 걸리고, 홍수가 나서 논밭이 무너져 내리는 절망적인 상황으로 끝난다. 자연재해와 질병, 짝사랑했던 사람의 부재 등이 중첩되면서 '지하촌'의 현실이 더 부각된다.

1936년에 발표된 이 작품은 간도에서 항일무장투쟁이 약화되고, 국내에서도 진보적인 문학 단체인 카프가 해산되고, 전반적으로 일본의 식민 지배가 강화된 상황을 반영하고 있다. 따라서 작가는 현실을 변혁하려는 의지나 낙관적인 미래를 제시하기보다는 하층계급의 궁핍한 삶과 출구 없는 어두운 현실을 '있는 그대로' 세세하게 묘사하는 방법을 택했다. 소설 처음부터 마지막으로 갈수록 악화되는 주인공 칠성과 가족의 상황을 독자에게 혐오감을 불러일으킬 정도로 사실적으로 그리고 있는 것이다. 이 부당하고 끔찍한 현실과 마주하려는 작가의 고발정신이 이념이나 시대가 변화한 것과 상관없이 이 작품이 아직도 읽히는 이유라 할 수 있다.

하지만 인간으로 견디기 힘든 가난 속에서도 비인간

who is wandering around after an industrial accident suffered during his factory laborer days, their sympathy and anger do not result in self-awareness or action. This short story ends on an utterly dismal tone, with a description of Ch'ilsŏng's despair following Kŭnnyŏn's departure, all of the village children catching an infectious eye disease, and all their farms and fields being flooded. This overlapping of the loss of a loved one, disease, and a natural disaster highlights the utter darkness of an underground village.

Published in 1936, "The Underground Village" reflects the ever-worsening reality of the time: the armed anti-Japanese struggle in Jiandao was weakened, and Japanese colonial rule intensified within the Korean Peninsula after the Japanese invasion of Manchuria in 1931 and the forced dissolution of KAPF, a progressive literary organization. Kang chose to describe the wretched lives of the underprivileged and their hopeless reality as faithfully as possible, rather than envisioning a will to change their reality or any sort of optimism for the future. The reality in which Ch'ilsŏng and the other characters in this story live deteriorates from beginning to the end, almost to the point of forcing readers

화되지 않은, 인간미가 너무도 풍부한 인물들이 당시 한국 실상의 비참함을 상쇄하고 있다는 점을 간과해서는 안 된다. 이 작품의 어머니는 인간으로 감당하기 어려운 극도의 가난과 질병 그리고 자식들에 대한 염려 속에서도 운명에 순종하며 자식들을 위해 온몸을 기꺼이 바친다. 형인 칠성이와 동생인 칠운이도 기본적 생존 욕구가 충족되지 않는 삶 때문에 서로가 원망스러울 때도 있지만 그들의 존재의 바탕에는 서로를 그리워하고 불쌍히 여기는 마음이 있다. 단편적으로 등장하는 동네 사람 개똥이 어머니도 자기 농사일을 팽개치고 해산하는 이웃을 업어다 뒷바라지를 해주고, 가혹한 가난에 신체적 장애까지 겹친 큰년이도 올곧고 의사가 분명하다. 이토록 참담한 역경 속에서도 인간미를 간직한 인물들은 모두 안쓰럽기 그지없으면서도 존경스럽기까지 하다.

to detest the story's descriptions themselves. Nevertheless, we also cannot overlook the fact that the characters in this short story counterbalance the wretchedness of the colonial Chosun reality with their warm hearts. The mother in the story, who has to struggle under a fate as harsh as any that fell to the lot of a human being, sustains it with unsparing labor and infinite maternal affection. And Kaettong's mother, a minor character in the story who is as poor as all the rest of them, stops tending her field and looks after her neighbor in her delivery, carrying her to her home on her back. The brothers Ch'ilsŏng and Ch'il-un bicker and hate each other now and then, but there is a stronger undercurrent of attachment between them that sustain them as a family. Kŭnnyŏn, on top of dire poverty, has the added misfortune of being blind, but she is upright and speaks her mind clearly. In the end, Kang's brave authorial spirit in facing and condemning this unjust and wretched reality must be why this work is still widely read and appreciated, regardless of the different time and ideological undertones.

비평의 목소리

Critical Acclaim

당대의 여성 작가들이 대부분 조선 문화의 중심지인 서울에서 살며, 더욱이 잡지사나 신문사의 기자로서 문단의 중심에 있으면서 작품 활동 바깥의 부수적인 활동에 더 바빴던 경우가 많았던 것에 비해 문단의 변두리이지만 당시 항일무장투쟁의 중심지인 간도에서 살면서 창작에 전념한 것이 작가 강경애에게 예술적으로나 정치적으로 긴장감을 주었고, 그러한 긴장감에서 당대 어느 작가보다 뛰어난 예술적 성취를 이룰 수 있었다. (……) 강경애는 보기 드물게 하층 여성의 목소리를 공식 기록으로 끌어 올린 식민지 시대 하층 여성의 대변자였고 민족 갈등, 계급 갈등이 첨예한 간도 지방의 항

Kang Kyŏng-ae devoted herself to writing while living in Jiandao, on the margin of Korean literary world, and one of the centers of the armed anti-Japanese struggle. Many other female authors of the time lived in Seoul, the center of the Korean literary and cultural worlds, and were busy with activities other than writing. Due to her marginalized position, Kang Kyŏng-ae was under stronger aesthetic and political pressure, which ultimately resulted in a higher level of artistic achievement in her works than in those of other authors. [...] Kang Kyŏng-ae was a rare champion of the lower class women during Korea's colonial period, giving them

일무장투쟁에 참가한 사람들의 면모를 목격하고, 그들의 고통과 정당성을 기록으로 증언하고, 그것을 일제의 직접 지배를 받는 식민지 조선에 전하는 것을 작가로서의 의무로 삼았다.

이상경, 『강경애—문학에서의 성과 계급』, 건국대학교출판부, 1997

1930년대 후반에서 「지하촌」의 인물들의 삶은 그들만의 특별한 것이 아니라 식민지 조선에서의 일상적인 생활이었다. 실제로 거리에는 많은 유랑민들이 있었고 그들은 칠성이처럼 하루하루 구걸로 목숨을 이어나갈 수밖에 없었다. 그런데 그러한 현실이 특별히 어둡고 폐쇄된 지하촌에 사는 불구자들이라는 극단적 상황 속의 인물들을 통해 묘사될 때 가장 궁핍한 시대로서의 식민지 조선의 본질이 뚜렷하게 드러나게 되는 것이다.

이상경, 『강경애—문학에서의 성과 계급』, 건국대학교출판부, 1997

강경애 소설 속의 하위 주체들, 특히 말을 잃은, 눈먼 존재인 하층계급 여성들은 여전히 뚜렷한 자신의 정체성을 주장하지 못한다. 그러나 계급 서사로 흡수되지 않는 그들의 삶은 도무지 결합되지 않는 애정 서사로,

a voice in the official media. She also thought it her authorial duty to record and testify to the difficult and righteous lives of participants in the armed anti-Japanese struggle in Jiandao (a scene of sharp class and national conflicts) and to deliver this knowledge to colonial Chosun, which was under direct Japanese rule.

Lee Sang-kyeong, *Kang Kyŏng-ae: Gender and Class in Literature* (Seoul: Konkuk University Press, 1997)

The kind of life led by residents of the "The Underground Village" was not specific to them, but typical of the everyday lives of most colonial Chosun subjects during the late 1930s. There were many vagrants on the street who had to beg to survive. In fact, Kang Kyŏng-ae's description of disabled characters living in an extremely squalid, dark, and confined village is a very effective tool to symbolically convey the impoverished nature of colonial Chosŭn.

Lee Sang-kyeong, *Kang Kyŏng-ae: Gender and Class in Literature* (Seoul: Konkuk University Press, 1997)

Subalterns in Kang Kyŏng-ae's works, especially those who lost their sight and tongues, do not have

혹은 서사의 과정에서 낯설게 출몰하는 이미지로 서사 속에 흔적을 남긴다. 가혹한 자기반성으로 그들의 몸을 얻고자 했던 식민지 여성 작가 강경애의 문학은 이 흔적 속에서 새로운 의미를 부여받을 수 있을 것이다.

서영인, 「강경애 문학의 여성성」, 김인환 외 편,
『강경애, 시대와 문학』, 랜덤하우스코리아, 2006

강경애의 궁핍묘사는 곧 작가의 세계관과 사상적 방향을 보여주는 것이다. 그는 초기에서 후기로 갈수록 궁핍묘사의 강도를 높이고 있는데 궁핍묘사의 중심을 이루는 것이 '먹는' 묘사이다. 강경애는 감각적 묘사에 출중하다. 시각, 청각, 후각, 촉각 등 감각적 묘사를 통해 묘사하고자 하는 대상을 생동감 있고 실감나게 표현해 낸다. (……) 감각 묘사에 탁월한 기법을 보인 강경애가 유독 미각 묘사에 있어서만은 감각적 묘사를 보여주지 않을 뿐 아니라 후기에 갈수록 먹는다는 일을 저주받은 상황으로 그리고 있음은 무엇을 뜻하겠는가. 이는 강경애가 식민지 현실의 궁핍을 가장 문제 삼고 있으며 이 궁핍한 현실은 갈수록 더욱 비참해지고 있음을 드러내려 한 것이다. (……) 그는 프로문학의 공식인 창작 방

the ability to claim their identities. Although they were not able to express themselves in life, we see their legacy through narratives of impossible love and strangely haunting images. Kang Kyŏng-ae, a female author during the colonial period who harshly criticized her own efforts to embody these subalterns, has acquired a new significance over time because of the traces of these people preserved through her works.

Seo Yeong-in, "Womanhood in Kang Kyŏng-ae's Literature," in Kim In-hwan, et. al. ed., *Kang Kyŏng-ae: Her Times and Literature* (Seoul: Random House Korea, 2006)

Kang Kyŏng-ae's depiction of poverty demonstrates her worldview and ideology. The level of poverty depicted in her works intensified as her writing career progressed, and her description of the act of eating lay at its center. Kang Kyŏng-ae had an excellent descriptive power when it came to sensations. She could realistically describe anything through her sensory descriptions, mobilizing all of her readers' senses, including sight, hearing, smell, and touch. [...] However, Kang Kyŏng-ae did not generally describe the sense of taste. Gradually, Kang's works connect eating with increasingly

법을 따르지 않고도 자신의 궁핍 체험을 묘사함으로써 자신의 세계관을 나타내 '빈궁소설'에 성공한 작가이다.

서정자, 「체험의 소설화, 강경애의 글쓰기 방식」, 『여성문학연구』 13호, 한국여성문학학회, 2005

강경애는 여성 개인의 생물학적 조건으로서의 모성이 아니라 사회적 의미를 지닌 모성을 그리면서도, 항상 구체적인 몸이라는 경로를 거쳐 형상화함으로써 현실성을 확보한다. (……) '지하촌'이라는 제목에 상응하는 비위생적이고 궁핍한 주거공간, 여성과 아이들, 신체적 기형을 지닌 이들과 같은 주변성의 상징들이 중첩되면서 식민지 현실이 가감 없이 드러나는 것이다. 그 중심에 여성의 현실, 엄밀하게는 어머니의 현실이 있다. (……) 어머니의 몸은 깨끗하고 풍요롭기는커녕 피가 흐르고, 자기 몸과 분리된 듯한 이질적인 '살덩이'를 품고 살아야 하는 비체화(卑體化, abject)된 몸이다. 노동과 출산으로 인해 피폐해진 이 어머니의 몸은 재생산 역할을 담당하는 여성의 실제 몸에 대한 사실적인 인식을 보여준다.

김양선, 「강경애 후기 소설과 체험의 윤리학—이산과 모성 체험을 중

wretched, condemnable situations. Through this, she meant to represent and condemn the destitute colonial reality, which was worsening by the day. [...] Although Kang did not adopt the "official" proletariat literary dogma, she succeeded in creating "poverty literature," which reflected her ideology through a description that was firmly based on her own experience with poverty.

Seo Jeong-ja, "Turning One's Experience into Fiction: Kang Kyŏng-ae's Creative Methods," *Yŏsŏng Munhak Yŏn'gu* 13 (2005).

Kang Kyŏng-ae depicts maternity not in a biological but a sociological sense, and imbues it with reality through concrete descriptions of the female body. [...] "The Underground Village" faithfully reveals colonial reality through overlapping benchmarks of marginalization, such as unhygienic and wretched living spaces, and the harsh lives of women, children, and the disabled. At the center of it all, there is women's reality or, more strictly speaking, mothers' reality. [...] Far from being clean or abundant, a mother's body is an abject body shedding blood; a body that is forced to embrace heterogeneous flesh seemingly separated from her

심으로」, 『여성문학연구』 11호, 한국여성문학학회, 2004

own body. This body of a mother, devastated by physical labor and childbirth, represents the author's view of the woman's body as primarily serving as a vessel for human reproduction.

Kim Yang-sun, "Kang Kyŏng-ae's Later Works and Ethics of Experience: With a Focus on the Experience of Dispersion and Maternity," *Yŏsŏng Munhak Yŏn'gu* 1 (2004).

강경애

식민지 노동 현실을 그려낸 수작으로 평가받는 『인간문제』의 작가 강경애. 강경애는 1906년 4월 20일 황해도 송화에서 가난한 농민의 딸로 태어났다. 4살 되던 해에 아버지가 돌아가시고나서 끼니를 거를 정도로 가난해지자, 5살 되던 해인 1910년 그녀의 어머니는 이웃 장연에 사는 최도감에게 개가를 한다. 강경애도 어머니를 따라 장연으로 이주하여 성장하게 된다. 여덟 살 무렵, 의붓아버지가 보다가 던져놓은 『춘향전』에서 한글을 깨쳐 『삼국지』 『숙향전』 같은 구소설을 독파하고, 동네사람들에게 불려 다니며 소설을 읽어주면서 '도토리 소설쟁이'란 별명을 얻게 된다. 처음으로 작가가 이야기 형식을 접하고 흥미를 느끼게 된 계기가 되었다.

열 살이 지나서야 장연소학교에 입학한 그는 여전히 학비와 학용품조차 마련하기 힘들어서 온갖 고통 속에서 눈치껏 공부를 하며 어렵게 학업을 마친다. 이때의 참담했던 경험은 강경애의 작품세계를 관류하는 궁핍과 제도적 모순에 대한 저항의식으로 표출된다.

Kang Kyŏng-ae

Kang Kyŏng-ae was born into a very poor family in Songhwa, Hwanghae-do in 1906. After her father died when she was only four, the family's survival was threatened. Her mother remarried Officer Ch'oe of Jangyeon, a neighboring town, and took Kang Kyŏng-ae with her. When she was eight, Kang Kyŏng-ae taught herself to read by reading her stepfather's copy of *Ch'unhyangjŏn*. She proceeded to read pre-modern novels like *Records of the Three Kingdoms* and *Sukhyangjŏn*, and read them to villagers at their invitation, earning the nickname "Acorn Storyteller." Kang Kyŏng-ae remembered this as the period when she became acquainted with and interested in literature.

Kang entered Jangyeon Elementary School when she was ten, but had a hard time continuing and finishing her elementary education because of her family's poverty. Her experience of poverty during this period stayed with her throughout her literary career, appearing in her novels and short stories as descriptions of poverty and condemnations of sys-

1921년 열다섯 살 무렵 의붓아버지가 죽은 뒤 형부의 도움으로 평양 숭의여학교에 진학한다. 이때도 가난하기는 매일반이어서 빠듯한 학비로 기숙사 생활을 해야 했고, 월사금을 못 무는 때도 있었다. 여학교 3학년 때인 1923년 그녀는 기숙사의 지나친 규칙에 항의하는 동맹휴학에 관련되어 퇴학을 당한다. 같은 해 고향 장연에 문학 강연을 온 양주동을 만나면서 본격적인 문학 수업을 시작한다. 이듬해 1924년 봄 강경애는 양주동을 따라 상경하여 양주동이 주관하던 '금성'사에 같이 기거하면서 문학공부를 하는 한편, 동덕여학교 3학년에 편입하여 1년간 공부했다. 하지만 이 해 가을 두 사람은 헤어지게 되는데 이유가 무엇인지는 알 수 없다. 다만 양주동이 그가 생래적으로 터득한 사회인식과는 다른 기질과 생각을 지녔기 때문인 것으로 추측된다.

양주동과 헤어진 후 그는 장연으로 내려와 언니(의붓언니)가 경영하는 서산여관에 기거하였다. 1920년대 후반 강경애는 주로 장연에 거주하면서 무산아동을 위한 '흥풍야학교'를 개설, 직접 학생들을 가르쳤다. 하지만 양주동과의 연애, 서울로 출분했던 사실 때문에 고향 사람들과 가족의 비난을 받자 1년 반 정도 간도로 가서

temic ills.

With her brother-in-law's help, Kang entered Sungui Girls School in 1921, when she was around fifteen, but still had a hard time paying for tuition and dorm expenses. In 1923, she was expelled from school because of her participation in a student strike protesting extremely strict dorm rules.

The same year, she met Yang Chu-dong, a young poet and literary scholars who was later to be a reigning literary critic, in Jangyeon, where he came to give a lecture about literature, and began to pursue a literary career herself. Kang went to Seoul in 1924 and studied for a year at Dongduk Girls School while living with Yang Chu-dong. She left Yang in fall of the same year, presumably because he wasn't exactly sympathetic to her sense of social justice.

She returned home to Jangyeon and established and taught at Hongpung Night School while staying at her stepsister's inn. Unable to fend off her family's and others' condemnation of her previous unmarried cohabitation with Yang Chu-dong, she moved to Jiandao and wandered throughout the Longjiang area as a part-time instructor. A year and a half later, she returned to Jangyeon once again. While

용정 일대에서 교육기관의 강사 노릇도 하고 특정한 직업 없이 지내다 다시 장연으로 돌아온다. 1929년에는 근우회(근우회는 1927년 5월 27일 창립된 전국적인 여성대중조직으로서 좌파 여성운동가들의 주도하에 '반제반봉건운동'을 전개했지만, 1931년 무렵 해산된 단체이다) 장연지회 회원으로 활동하기도 했다. 1931년 1월 《조선일보》 부인문예란에 단편 「파금」을 독자투고 형식으로 발표하며 등단하게 된다. 이 시기 양주동과의 만남, 근우회 활동은 소설가이자 여성으로서의 자아를 정립하는 데 중요한 역할을 했다.

같은 해 강경애는 장연군청 서기로 있던 장하일과 결혼하여 간도 용정으로 이주한다. 장하일은 용정의 동흥중학교 교사직으로 일하면서 항일무장투쟁과도 일정하게 연루되었던 것으로 보인다. 강경애는 집안일에 서툰 탓에 간혹 남편과 싸우기도 했으나, 그는 「원고 첫 낭독」과 「원고료 이백원」에서 볼 수 있듯이 강경애가 쓴 원고를 읽고 조언해 주는 훌륭한 독자였으며, 아내와 동지적 관계를 유지했던 것으로 보인다. 이후 강경애는 간도에 거주하면서 간도에 이주한 조선인의 참혹한 삶을 연이어 발표한다. 1934년 8월부터 12월까지 《동아일

working as a member of the Jangyeon Branch of Kŭnuhoe, a leftist women's organization established in 1929, she made her literary debut in January 1931 when her short story "Pagŭm [Broken Zither]" was published as a reader contribution in the *Chosun Ilbo* newspaper. Her relationship with Yang Chu-dong and her activity at the Kŭnuhoe played a significant role in establishing her identity as a novelist and self-awareness as a woman activist.

The same year, Kang married Chang Ha-il, a Jangyeon District Office clerk, and moved with him to Longjiang in Jindao. Chang Ha-il worked as a teacher at Donghong Middle School while, presumably, being involved with the armed anti-Japanese movement in the area. Although Kang sometimes argued with her husband about household chores, they enjoyed a harmonious camaraderie as glimpsed in her short stories such as "First Manuscript Reading" and "Two Hundred Won Writer's Fee." During her life in Jiandao, she continued to write short stories condemning the wretched living conditions of migrant Koreans and serialized *The Human Problem*, one of the most representative realism novels of the colonial period, in the *Donga Ilbo* newspaper between August and December

보》에 식민지 시대 리얼리즘 소설의 대표작으로 꼽히는 장편소설『인간문제』를 연재했다.

1936년부터 안수길, 박영준 등과 함께《북향》동인으로 활동하기도 했으나 건강 사정 때문에 적극적으로 활동하지는 못했다. 같은 해 3월「지하촌」을 발표했다. 1939년《조선일보》간도지국장을 지내기도 했던 그는 3년 전부터 얻은 병이 악화되어, 고향 장연으로 돌아온다. 1940년 2월에는 상경하여 경성제대병원에서 치료를 받기도 하고, 원산의 삼방 약수터를 다니기도 했으나 끝내 병이 악화되어 1944년 4월 26일 생을 마감한다.

1934.

Although Kang joined the *Pukhyang* coterie with authors like An Su-gil and Pak Yŏng-jun in 1936, she could not participate actively due to her deteriorating health. "The Underground Village" was published in March 1936. She moved back to Jangyeon in 1939 while working as the *Chosun Ilbo* Jiandao Branch chief, and, eventually, to Seoul in February 1940 in an attempt to have her illness treated. Although she was treated at the Gyeongseong Imperial University Hospital and tried the legendary healing waters of the Sambang Mineral Spring in Wonsan, she died in 1944.

번역 **서지문** Translated by Suh Ji-moon

1948년에 출생하여 이화여자대학교에서 영문학 학사를, 미국 뉴욕주립대학교에서 영문학 박사 학위를 받고 1978년부터 2013년에 정년퇴직하기까지 고려대학교 영문학과 교수로 35년간 재직했다. 여러 세기에 걸친 한국의 역사적 수난과 자신의 성장기였던 1950년대의 한국인들의 극심한 가난과 고통, 그리고 1960~70년대의 격변에 따른 사회갈등이 그녀에게 한국 민족의 고난사를 세계에 알리고 싶다는 열망을 심어주었고, 석사 학위를 취득한 이후 강의를 하는 한편으로 한국문학 영역 작업을 수행하게 했다. 그녀의 노력은 한국 현대문학의 태동기로부터 1990년대까지의 대표 단편 선집인 『The Rainy Spell and Other Korean Short Stories』 (M. E. Sharpe, 1993), 1970~90년대의 국가 근대화에 수반한 고민을 담은 7편의 중편 선집인 『The Golden Phoenix: Seven Contemporary Korean Short Storeis』 (Lynne Rienner, 1996), 분단의 아픔을 절제된 언어로 극명하게 표현한 『The Descendants of Cain』 (황순원 작 『카인의 후예』, M. E. Sharpe, 1997) 등으로 결실을 맺었다. 『Brother Enemy: Poems of the Korean War』 (White Pine, 2002)는 한국전쟁 당시에 전선과 후방에서 씌어진 군인과 민간인들의 삶과 죽음을 읊은 시들을 모은 시집이고 『The House with a Sunken Courtyard』 (김원일 작 『마당 깊은 집』, Dalky Archive Press, 2013)은 한국전쟁이 한국인의 삶과 심성에 남긴 후유증을 작가의 어린 시절의 직접 경험을 통해 조망한 장편이다. 『Remembering the Forgotten War』 (M. E. Sharpe, 2001)는 미국 몬태나대학교 맨스필드연구소와 공동 집필, 편집한 한국전쟁 문학에 대한 연구서이다. 2000년대에 들어와서는 강의와 연구, 학회 활동, 보직 수행 등으로 영역 작업을 활발히 수행하지 못했으나 은퇴와 함께 본격적인 영역 작업을 계획하고 있다. 그리고 한국문학번역원에서 시상하는 2014년도 한국문학번역상 대상 수상은 그 목표를 향해 정진하기 위한 거대한 격려가 될 것임에 틀림없다.

Suh Ji-moon was born in 1948 and grew up mostly in Seoul. She received her B.A. from Ewha Womans University in Seoul and her advanced degrees in the U.S. Her childhood years spent in the indigent 1950s and her adolescence and young womanhood in the industrialization-democratization throes of the 1960s and 70s gave her a strong desire to serve her country and countrymen in some significant way.

Having chosen literature as her major field, she made it her mission to put Korean literature on the literary map of the world. She thought that the innumerable tribulations her compatriots have endured throughout history and the tragedy that dogged her country for many centuries were something that the world would do well to recognize and contemplate.

Her efforts have borne fruit in several anthologies and novels in English translation. Her first collection, on which she worked for more than ten years, *The Rainy Spell and Other Korean Stories* (Onyx Press, 1983, revised and enlarged edition by M. E. Sharpe, 1993), is a collection of fourteen Korean short stories from the beginning of 'modern' literature in Korea to the 1990s. *The Golden Phoenix: Seven Contemporary Korean Short Stories* (Lynne Rienner, 1996), contains seven lengthy short stories by the highest ranking Korean writers of the 1970s, 80s and 90s. The stories show Koreans trying to sort things out and keep their balance amid the rapid confluence of newly imported Western civilization and traditional ways and values. *The Descendants of Cain* is a quiet but powerful novel by the great master Hwang Sun-won, which recounts the writer's own perilous exodus from North Korea shortly after the nation's liberation in 1945 when the Russians began to move in and terror began to spread. And *Brother Enemy* (White Pine, 2002) is a collection of 108 poems from the Korean War days, many of them depicting the cruelties of war and the pain and helplessness of those caught in its maelstrom, and some quietly contemplating the absurdities of human nature and the meaning of history. *The House with a Sunken Courtyard* (Dalky archive Press, 2013), a Kim Won-il novel which vividly portrays the precarious lives of war refuges in the early 1950s, is her most recent effort.

The pressures of teaching duties and other scholarly and social activities have hindered her full devotion to translation, but, after her mandatory retirement in 2013, she plans to devote herself more fully to translating Korean literature to accomplish at mature years the self-elected mission of her youth. And the Korean Literary Translation Institute's grand prize in literary translation, awarded to her in 2014 for her translation of Kim Won-il's *The House with a Sunken Courtyard*, is sure to be a great encouragement toward that end.

바이링궐 에디션 한국 대표 소설 090
지하촌

2014년 11월 14일 초판 1쇄 발행

지은이 강경애 | 옮긴이 서지문 | 펴낸이 김재범
기획위원 정은경, 전성태, 이경재
편집 정수인, 이은혜, 김형욱, 윤단비 | 관리 박신영 | 디자인 이춘희
펴낸곳 (주)아시아 | 출판등록 2006년 1월 27일 제406-2006-000004호
주소 서울특별시 동작구 서달로 161-1(흑석동 100-16)
전화 02.821.5055 | 팩스 02.821.5057 | 홈페이지 www.bookasia.org
ISBN 979-11-5662-049-5 (set) | 979-11-5662-064-8 (04810)
값은 뒤표지에 있습니다.

Bi-lingual Edition Modern Korean Literature 090
The Underground Village

Written by Kang Kyŏng-ae | **Translated by** Suh Ji-moon
Published by Asia Publishers | 161-1, Seodal-ro, Dongjak-gu, Seoul, Korea
Homepage Address www.bookasia.org | **Tel**. (822).821.5055 | **Fax**. (822).821.5057
First published in Korea by Asia Publishers 2014
ISBN 979-11-5662-049-5 (set) | 979-11-5662-064-8 (04810)

바이링궐 에디션 한국 대표 소설

한국문학의 가장 중요하고 첨예한 문제의식을 가진 작가들의 대표작을 주제별로 선정!
하버드 한국학 연구원 및 세계 각국의 한국문학 전문 번역진이 참여한 번역 시리즈!
미국 하버드대학교와 컬럼비아대학교 동아시아학과, 캐나다 브리티시컬럼비아대학교 아시아학과 등 해외 대학에서 교재로 채택!

바이링궐 에디션 한국 대표 소설 set 1

분단 Division

01 병신과 머저리-**이청준** The Wounded-**Yi Cheong-jun**
02 어둠의 혼-**김원일** Soul of Darkness-**Kim Won-il**
03 순이삼촌-**현기영** Sun-i Samch'on-**Hyun Ki-young**
04 엄마의 말뚝 1-**박완서** Mother's Stake I-**Park Wan-suh**
05 유형의 땅-**조정래** The Land of the Banished-**Jo Jung-rae**

산업화 Industrialization

06 무진기행-**김승옥** Record of a Journey to Mujin-**Kim Seung-ok**
07 삼포 가는 길-**황석영** The Road to Sampo-**Hwang Sok-yong**
08 아홉 켤레의 구두로 남은 사내-**윤흥길** The Man Who Was Left as Nine Pairs of Shoes-**Yun Heung-gil**
09 돌아온 우리의 친구-**신상웅** Our Friend's Homecoming-**Shin Sang-ung**
10 원미동 시인-**양귀자** The Poet of Wŏnmi-dong-**Yang Kwi-ja**

여성 Women

11 중국인 거리-**오정희** Chinatown-**Oh Jung-hee**
12 풍금이 있던 자리-**신경숙** The Place Where the Harmonium Was-**Shin Kyung-sook**
13 하나코는 없다-**최윤** The Last of Hanak'o-**Ch'oe Yun**
14 인간에 대한 예의-**공지영** Human Decency-**Gong Ji-young**
15 빈처-**은희경** Poor Man's Wife-**Eun Hee-kyung**

바이링궐 에디션 한국 대표 소설 set 2

자유 Liberty

16 필론의 돼지-**이문열** Pilon's Pig-**Yi Mun-yol**
17 슬로우 불릿-**이대환** Slow Bullet-**Lee Dae-hwan**
18 직선과 독가스-**임철우** Straight Lines and Poison Gas-**Lim Chul-woo**
19 깃발-**홍희담** The Flag-**Hong Hee-dam**
20 새벽 출정-**방현석** Off to Battle at Dawn-**Bang Hyeon-seok**

사랑과 연애 Love and Love Affairs

21 별을 사랑하는 마음으로-**윤후명** With the Love for the Stars-**Yun Hu-myong**
22 목련공원-**이승우** Magnolia Park-**Lee Seung-u**
23 칼에 찔린 자국-**김인숙** Stab-**Kim In-suk**
24 회복하는 인간-**한강** Convalescence-**Han Kang**
25 트렁크-**정이현** In the Trunk-**Jeong Yi-hyun**

남과 북 South and North

26 판문점-**이호철** Panmunjom-**Yi Ho-chol**
27 수난 이대-**하근찬** The Suffering of Two Generations-**Ha Geun-chan**
28 분지-**남정현** Land of Excrement-**Nam Jung-hyun**
29 봄 실상사-**정도상** Spring at Silsangsa Temple-**Jeong Do-sang**
30 은행나무 사랑-**김하기** Gingko Love-**Kim Ha-kee**

바이링궐 에디션 한국 대표 소설 set 3

서울 Seoul

31 눈사람 속의 검은 항아리-**김소진** The Dark Jar within the Snowman-**Kim So-jin**
32 오후, 가로지르다-**하성란** Traversing Afternoon-**Ha Seong-nan**
33 나는 봉천동에 산다-**조경란** I Live in Bongcheon-dong-**Jo Kyung-ran**
34 그렇습니까? 기린입니다-**박민규** Is That So? I'm A Giraffe-**Park Min-gyu**
35 성탄특선-**김애란** Christmas Specials-**Kim Ae-ran**

전통 Tradition

36 무자년의 가을 사흘-**서정인** Three Days of Autumn, 1948-**Su Jung-in**
37 유자소전-**이문구** A Brief Biography of Yuja-**Yi Mun-gu**
38 향기로운 우물 이야기-**박범신** The Fragrant Well-**Park Bum-shin**
39 월행-**송기원** A Journey under the Moonlight-**Song Ki-won**
40 협죽도 그늘 아래-**성석제** In the Shade of the Oleander-**Song Sok-ze**

아방가르드 Avant-garde

41 아겔다마-**박상륭** Akeldama-**Park Sang-ryoong**
42 내 영혼의 우물-**최인석** A Well in My Soul-**Choi In-seok**
43 당신에 대해서-**이인성** On You-**Yi In-seong**
44 회색 時-**배수아** Time In Gray-**Bae Su-ah**
45 브라운 부인-**정영문** Mrs. Brown-**Jung Young-moon**

바이링궐 에디션 한국 대표 소설 set 4

디아스포라 Diaspora

46 속옷-**김남일** Underwear-**Kim Nam-il**
47 상하이에 두고 온 사람들-**공선옥** People I Left in Shanghai-**Gong Sun-ok**
48 모두에게 복된 새해-**김연수** Happy New Year to Everyone-**Kim Yeon-su**
49 코끼리-**김재영** The Elephant-**Kim Jae-young**
50 먼지별-**이경** Dust Star-**Lee Kyung**

가족 Family

51 혜자의 눈꽃-**천승세** Hye-ja's Snow-Flowers-**Chun Seung-sei**
52 아베의 가족-**전상국** Ahbe's Family-**Jeon Sang-guk**
53 문 앞에서-**이동하** Outside the Door-**Lee Dong-ha**
54 그리고, 축제-**이혜경** And Then the Festival-**Lee Hye-kyung**
55 봄밤-**권여선** Spring Night-**Kwon Yeo-sun**

유머 Humor

56 오늘의 운세-**한창훈** Today's Fortune-**Han Chang-hoon**
57 새-**전성태** Bird-**Jeon Sung-tae**
58 밀수록 다시 가까워지는-**이기호** So Far, and Yet So Near-**Lee Ki-ho**
59 유리방패-**김중혁** The Glass Shield-**Kim Jung-hyuk**
60 전당포를 찾아서-**김종광** The Pawnshop Chase-**Kim Chong-kwang**

바이링궐 에디션 한국 대표 소설 set 5

관계 Relationship

61 도둑견습 - **김주영** Robbery Training-**Kim Joo-young**
62 사랑하라, 희망 없이 - **윤영수** Love, Hopelessly-**Yun Young-su**
63 봄날 오후, 과부 셋 - **정지아** Spring Afternoon, Three Widows-**Jeong Ji-a**
64 유턴 지점에 보물지도를 묻다 - **윤성희** Burying a Treasure Map at the U-turn-**Yoon Sung-hee**
65 쁘이거나 쯔이거나 - **백가흠** Puy, Thuy, Whatever-**Paik Ga-huim**

일상의 발견 Discovering Everyday Life

66 나는 음식이다 - **오수연** I Am Food-**Oh Soo-yeon**
67 트럭 - **강영숙** Truck-**Kang Young-sook**
68 통조림 공장 - **편혜영** The Canning Factory-**Pyun Hye-young**
69 꽃 - **부희령** Flowers-**Pu Hee-ryoung**
70 피의일요일 - **윤이형** BloodySunday-**Yun I-hyeong**

금기와 욕망 Taboo and Desire

71 북소리 - **송영** Drumbeat-**Song Yong**

72 발칸의 장미를 내게 주었네 - **정미경** He Gave Me Roses of the Balkans-**Jung Mi-kyung**

73 아무도 돌아오지 않는 밤 - **김숨** The Night Nobody Returns Home-**Kim Soom**

74 젓가락여자 - **천운영** Chopstick Woman-**Cheon Un-yeong**

75 아직 일어나지 않은 일 - **김미월** What Has Yet to Happen-**Kim Mi-wol**